野性的呼喚

The Call of the Wild

原著 JACK LONDON
改寫 DAVID A. HILL
譯者 安卡斯

For the Student

 Listen to the story and do some activities on your Audio CD.

 Talk about the story.

For the Teacher

Go to our Readers Resource site for information on using readers and downloadable Resource Sheets, photocopiable Worksheets, and Tapescripts. www.helblingreaders.com

For lots of great ideas on using Graded Readers consult Reading Matters, the Teacher's Guide to using Helbling Readers.

Structures

Sequencing of future tenses	• Could / was able to / managed to
Present perfect plus yet, already, just	• Had to / didn't have to
First conditional	• Shall / could for offers
Present and past passive	• May / can / could for permission • Might for future possibility
How long?	• Make and let
Very / really / quite	• Causative have • Want / ask / tell someone to do something

Structures from lower levels are also included.

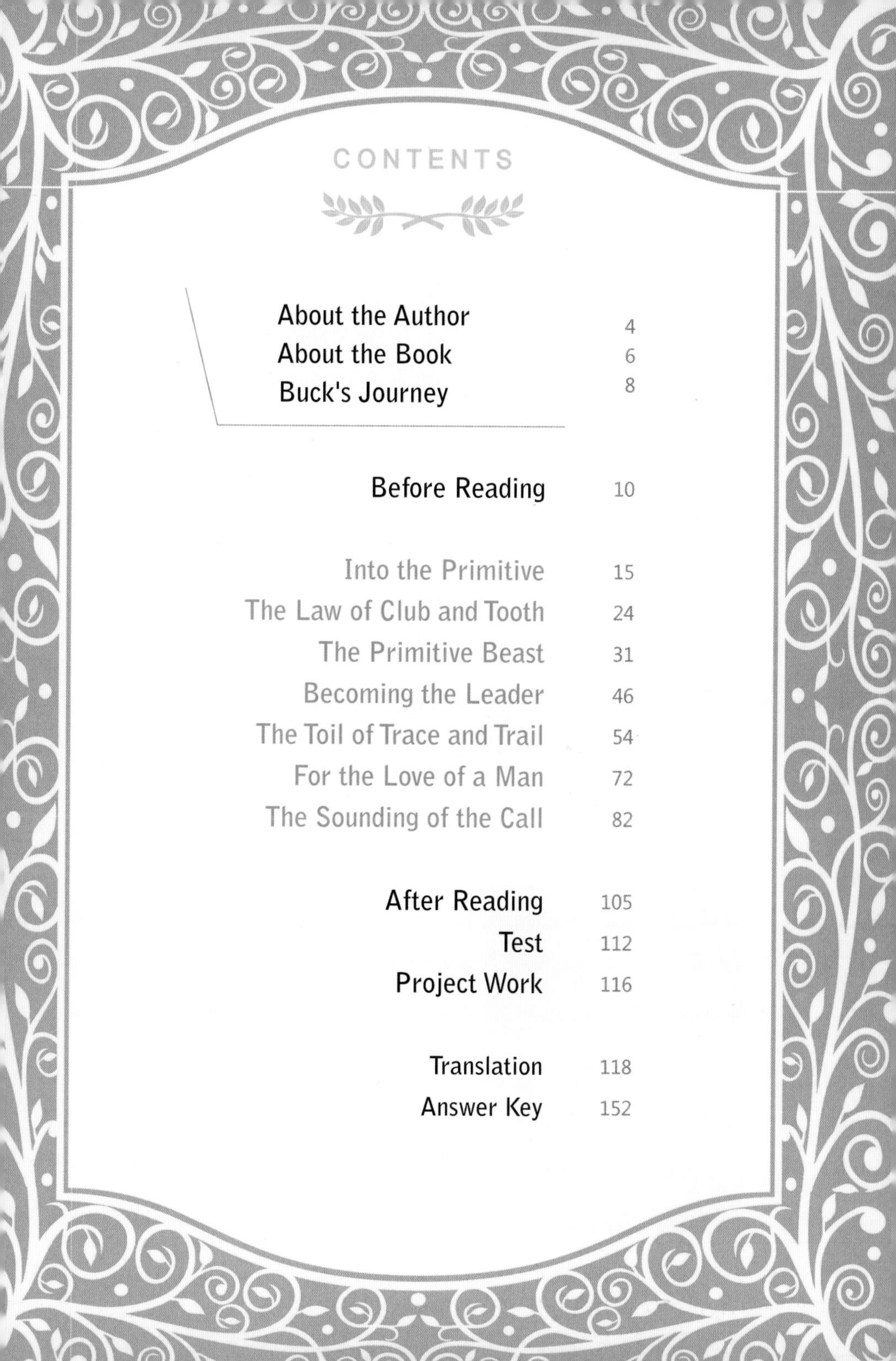

CONTENTS

About the Author

Jack London was born in San Francisco in 1876. Life was hard when Jack was growing up and he started working when he was 10. He did a variety of jobs, some legal[1], others not, and even spent some time living as a tramp[2]. In his free time he went to the library and spent many hours there reading.

In 1894 he went back to school, and published his first short story *Typhoon off the Coast of Japan*. Then in 1896 he went to the University of California, Berkeley, but had to leave because of money problems.

In July, 1897 he left for the Klondike Gold Rush[3] in Alaska. Like many others, he became very ill and came home and worked as a full-time writer. He wrote short stories and soon became successful.

In 1903 he wrote the story which made his name[4]: *The Call of the Wild*. His next novel was *The Sea-Wolf* (1904). With his earnings[5] he bought a large farm in California, where he died in 1916.

London was a prolific[6] writer. Between 1905 and 1916 he published 18 novels and six collections of short stories, as well as a play and various works of non-fiction[7], including a biography[8]. Other works were published after his death.

His most famous novels were *White Fang*[9] (1906), *The Iron Heel* (1908) and *Martin Eden* (1909). However, he was criticized[10] for his writing technique in later life: he took pieces written by other people in news reports, etc. and changed them to his own style. Some people felt it was plagiarism[11].

1 legal [ˋligḷ] (a.) 合法的
2 tramp [træmp] (n.) 遊民
3 Klondike Gold Rush，1890 年代加拿大育空地區的克朗代克淘金熱潮，道森市是當時的輻輳城市
4 make one's name 揚名
5 earnings [ˋɝnɪŋz] (n.) 收入
6 prolific [prəˋlɪfɪk] (a.) 多產的
7 non-fiction [nɑnˋfɪkʃən] (n.) 非小說類文學
8 biography [ˋbaɪˏɑgrəfɪ] (n.) 傳記
9 fang [fæŋ] (n.) 牙；犬齒
10 criticize [ˋkrɪtəˏsaɪz] (v.) 批評
11 plagiarism [ˋpledʒəˏrɪzəm] (n.) 抄襲

About the Book

The Call of the Wild (1903) is considered by many people to be Jack London's finest piece of writing, and it is widely recognized[1] as one of the classics of American literature.

The main character of the story is Buck, a large dog, who is stolen from his comfortable life in California and sold as a sled[2] dog in the frozen[3] Klondike. Buck's new life is harsh[4] and cruel and he is forced to learn to adapt[5] in order to survive[6]. He works in a team of dogs pulling sleds loaded with mail for the gold prospectors[7] who have rushed[8] to the cold north.

Buck is strong and determined[9] and soon becomes the leader. Throughout the book, as Buck passes through the hands of various owners, he grows closer and closer to his primitive[10] origins and the "call of the wild" becomes stronger and stronger.

The story explores[11] a number of themes which were dear to London. London took a copy of Charles Darwin's *The Origin of the Species*[12] with him when he went to the Klondike and the story strongly reflects Darwin's theory of the 'survival of the fittest'. This law of the survival of the fittest applies[13] to both the animal and human worlds: both men and animals need to use their strength and intelligence to survive.

London was a determinist[14] and believed that our lives are conditioned[15] by what we inherit[16] and the environment which surrounds us. So when Buck lives with Judge Miller he is a pet and lives an easy, peaceful life. His deeper inherited instincts[17] do not appear until he moves to an environment that allows them to develop. These themes[18] are revisited in London's later novel *White Fang*.

1 recognize [ˋrɛkəg͵naɪz] (v.) 認定；認可
2 sled [slɛd] (n.) 雪橇
3 frozen [ˋfrozn̩] (a.) 冰凍的；極冷的
4 harsh [hɑrʃ] (a.) 嚴酷的
5 adapt [əˋdæpt] (v.) 適應
6 survive [sɚˋvaɪv] (v.) 活下來
7 prospector [ˋprɑspɛktɚ] (n.) 探礦者
8 rush [rʌʃ] (v.) 奔赴
9 determined [dɪˋtɝmɪnd] (a.) 果斷的；堅決的
10 primitive [ˋprɪmətɪv] (a.) 原始的
11 explore [ɪkˋsplor] (v.) 探索
12 species [ˋspiʃiz] (n.) 物種
13 apply [əˋplaɪ] (v.) 應用
14 determinist [dɪˋtɝmɪnɪst] (n.) 因果決定論者
15 condition [kənˋdɪʃən] (v.) 決定
16 inherit [ɪnˋhɛrɪt] (v.) 繼承
17 instinct [ˋɪnstɪŋkt] (n.) 本能
18 theme [θim] (n.) 主題；題材

The Yukon Territory

BUCK'S JOURNEY

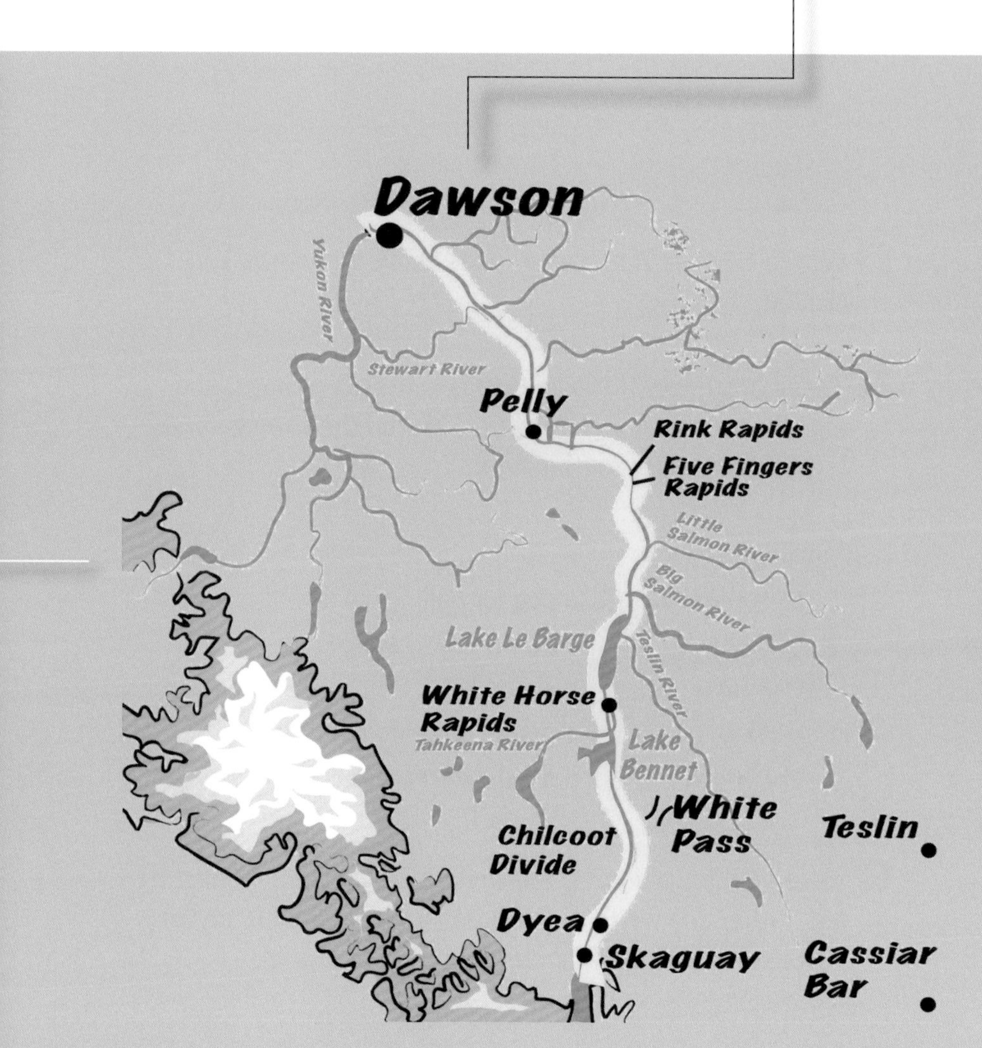

Before Reading

1 What do you know about dogs? Circle the words in the box which can best be used to describe them.

Carnivorous	Undependable	Friendly
Herbivorous	Dangerous	Useful
Intelligent	Wild	Loyal
Faithful	Domesticated	Strong

2 With a partner make sentences using the words you circled.

3 There are many different kinds (breeds) of dogs, and each breed has a different use. Match the breeds on the left with the uses on the right.

1 Alsatian	a a lap-dog, to be petted
2 St Bernard	b a dog for pulling sleds in the snow
3 Pointer	c a guard dog or police dog
4 Pekinese	d a sheepdog
5 Husky	e a gun dog, for hunting
6 Collie	f a mountain rescue dog

4 Have you got a dog? If so, write a paragraph about it. If not, either (a) write about a dog you know well, or (b) write what you think about dogs.

5 Answer these questions:

(a) What country does Alaska belong to?
(b) Where is Alaska located?
(c) What is the climate like?
(d) What wild animals live there?
(e) Who were the first inhabitants of Alaska?

6 Why did Alaska suddenly become famous at the end of the 19th century? Tick (✓) below.

- ☐ The film industry started there.
- ☐ People discovered gold there.
- ☐ Men started digging for oil.
- ☐ Ice-cream was invented there.

7 If you were going on a trip to Alaska what things would you want to take with you? Make a list under the two headings.

CLOTHES	EQUIPMENT

8 Would you like to live in or visit Alaska? Why/why not? Tell a partner.

9 Look at this picture of a husky. Write a description of it. Think about its size, shape and color. What wild animal does it look like?

10 Think of another animal you like. Describe it to a partner. Can they guess its name?

2 **11** Listen and Match. The story is about a dog called Buck who first lives in California, and then is stolen and taken to Alaska. Listen to these extracts from the story. Then match them to the pictures below.

12 In pairs decide a title for each picture. Then choose one and describe it in detail. Add as much information as you can. Think of what is happening in each picture.

13 The titles of the chapters show us something about the changes in Buck's life and in his character. Match the chapter titles on the left with the descriptions on the right.

1	Into the Primitive	a	Buck discovers that in order to survive he must become the best dog.
2	The Law of Club and Tooth	b	Buck finally finds a man whom he respects and who respects him.
3	The Primitive Beast	c	In the new world, Buck has to deal with violence every day. The violence of men with their weapons, and dogs with their teeth.
4	Becoming the Leader	d	Buck leaves his comfortable life and is introduced into an older and more savage world.
5	The Toil of Trace and Trail	e	As Buck gets closer to the wild and primitive world of his ancestors, he increasingly feels close to nature.
6	For the Love of a Man	f	Animals are different in this new world. They have older and more natural laws and instincts.
7	The Sounding of the Call	g	Buck learns to work as a sled-dog. It is hard work and he must work with the dogs in a team pulling a heavy sled across tracks in the snow.

INTO THE PRIMITIVE

Buck did not read the newspapers. So he did not know that there was trouble ahead. Trouble for every dog with strong muscles and warm long hair, from Seattle to southern California. Some men had found a yellow metal in the Arctic[1] darkness, and thousands of[2] other men were rushing there. These men wanted dogs that were heavy, with strong muscles for working hard and furry[3] coats to protect them from the cold.

Buck lived at a big house in a sunny valley in California which was owned by Judge[4] Miller. And Buck ruled over it all. He was born there, and had lived there for the four years of his life. There were many other dogs, but they lived together in the kennels[5], or inside the house. But Buck was neither a house dog nor a kennel dog. The whole of Judge Miller's land was his. Buck was king – king over all the creeping[6] crawling[7], flying things of Judge Miller's lands, humans included.

His father, Elmo, a huge St Bernard, had been the judge's inseparable[8] companion[9]. And when he died, Buck took his father's place. He was not so large – he weighed only sixty kilograms – for his mother, Shep, had been a Scottish sheepdog. He had had a good life and he was proud of himself, for he had not become a house dog. Hunting and other outdoor activities had hardened[10] his muscles, and swimming had made him healthy.

1 Arctic [`ɑrktɪk] (a.) 北極的
2 thousands of 數千的
3 furry [`fɝɪ] (a.) 覆有毛皮的
4 judge [dʒʌdʒ] (n.) 法官
5 kennel [`kɛnl̩] (n.) 狗舍
6 creep [krip] (v.) 躡手躡足地走
7 crawl [krɔl] (v.) 爬行
8 inseparable [ɪn`sɛpərəbl̩] (a.) 形影不離的
9 companion [kəm`pænjən] (n.) 同伴
10 harden [`hɑrdn̩] (v.) 使變硬

4 This was Buck in the autumn of 1897, when the discovery of gold in the Klondike brought men from everywhere to the frozen north. But Buck did not read the newspapers. And he did not know that Manuel, one of the gardener's helpers, was not a good man. Manuel gambled[1] and wasted the little money he had. And one time when the judge was away on business, and his sons were busy with an athletics[2] club, Manuel did something terrible. No one saw him and Buck go off on what Buck thought was a walk. No one saw them arrive at the railway station, where Manuel sold Buck to a man who was waiting for him.

Manuel put a rope[3] round Buck's neck, under his collar[4]. Buck accepted this because he knew Manuel, but when the rope was given to another man, he growled[5] dangerously. And when the rope was tightened round his neck, he started to choke[6] and jumped at the man in anger.

The man fought him off and forced Buck to lie on his back, and tightened the rope even more. Buck had never been treated so badly[7] in his life, and he had never been so angry. Then his strength drained[8] away and he soon became unconscious[9]. He was still unconscious when the train arrived and the two men threw him into the baggage car.

1 gamble [ˋgæmbḷ] (v.) 賭博
2 athletics [æθˋlɛtɪks] (n.) 體育運動
3 rope [rop] (n.) 繩子
4 collar [ˋkɑlɚ] (n.) 頸圈
5 growl [graʊl] (v.) 嗥叫；咆哮
6 choke [tʃok] (v.) 窒息；哽噎
7 be treated so badly 被虐待
8 drain [dren] (v.) 耗盡
9 unconscious [ʌnˋkɑnʃəs] (a.) 不省人事的
10 whistle [ˋhwɪsḷ] (n.) 哨子

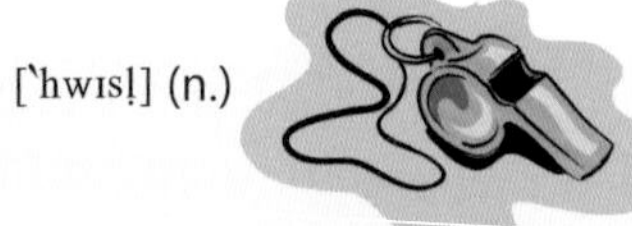

11 kidnap [ˋkɪdnæp] (v.) 綁架
12 wrap [ræp] (v.) 覆蓋
13 waterfront [ˋwɔtɚˏfrʌnt] (n.) 濱水區
14 barman [ˋbɑrmən] (n.) 酒吧店主
15 daze [dez] (v.) 使眩惑；使昏迷
16 brass [bræs] (a.) 黃銅製的

TRUST

- Buck goes with Manuel because he trusts him, but Manuel betrays Buck's trust. Who do you trust? Has anyone ever betrayed your trust?

When he woke up he heard a whistle[10] blow, and he knew where he was because he had often traveled by train with the judge. He opened his eyes, and he was filled with the full anger of a kidnapped[11] king. The man jumped for the rope, but Buck was too quick for him. He closed his teeth on the man's hand, and held on until he was choked unconscious again.

Later the man, his hand wrapped[12] in a bloody handkerchief, and his right trouser leg torn from knee to ankle, went into a San Francisco bar on the Waterfront[13]. He talked to the barman[14].

Buck was dazed[15] with horrible pains in his throat and on his tongue. He was thrown down and choked repeatedly, until they managed to cut the brass[16] collar off his neck. Then the rope was removed and he was pushed into a cage.

6

He lay there for the rest of the night, feeling angry. He could not understand what it all meant. What did these strange men want with him? Why were they keeping him in this small box? He felt worried that something bad was going to happen to him soon. He jumped up several times in the night, expecting to see the judge or his sons come in, but each time it was only the barman checking on him.

Buck passed through many hands[1] in that cage. He traveled by wagon[2] and ferry[3] boat with other boxes to the railway station, where he was put on an express train[4]. For two days and nights he traveled north, without food and drink. And all the time Buck grew more and more angry. He was desperate[5] for a drink to ease[6] his swollen[7] throat and tongue. But he decided that nobody would ever put a rope around his neck again. His anger would be directed against the first person who tried to hurt him. His eyes became red, and he changed into a raging[8] devil[9]. He was so changed that the judge would not have recognized him.

After two days he was carried off the train in Seattle into a small, high-walled yard. There a fat man in a red sweater broke open the cage with a small axe[10], while holding a club[11] in the other hand. When there was a big enough opening, Buck jumped out like a red-eyed devil, straight at the fat man.

1 pass through many hands 輾轉經過許多人的手
2 wagon [ˋwægən] (n.) 運貨馬車
3 ferry [ˋfɛrɪ] (n.) 渡輪
4 express train 特快車
5 desperate [ˋdɛspərɪt] (a.) 情急拼命的
6 ease [iz] (v.) 緩和
7 swollen [ˋswolən] (a.) 浮腫的
8 raging [ˋredʒɪŋ] (a.) 憤怒的
9 devil [ˋdɛvḷ] (n.) 惡魔
10 axe [æks] (n.) 斧頭

11 club [klʌb] (n.) 球棒；棍棒

7 But in mid-air, just as his teeth were going to close on the man, he received a shock that he had never felt before. It turned him over and onto the ground. He had never been struck[1] by a club in his life, and he did not understand. With a bark[2] that was more a scream[3] he jumped at the man again, and again he was clubbed[4] to the ground. Although he now knew what was happening to him, his anger made him continue jumping. He was smashed[5] down a dozen times.

In the end he could jump no more. Blood was flowing from his nose, mouth and ears. The man came and deliberately[6] hit him hard on the nose. It was agony[7] for Buck. With a roar[8] like a lion, he jumped at the man again, but the man hit him under the jaw[9]. Buck rose into the air then crashed[10] to the ground on his head and chest. For the last time he rushed at the man but the man struck him with a clever blow[11] and Buck fell down unconscious.

'He's a great dog-breaker,' said one of the men who'd carried Buck into the yard.

Buck's senses[12] came back to him, but not his strength. He lay where he had fallen, and watched the man in the red sweater.

"Answers to the name of Buck," said the fat man, reading the barman's letter. 'Well, Buck, we've had our little fight, and the best thing we can do is stop there. You've learned your place. Be a good dog and it'll go well for you. Be a bad dog, and I'll beat you again. Understand?'

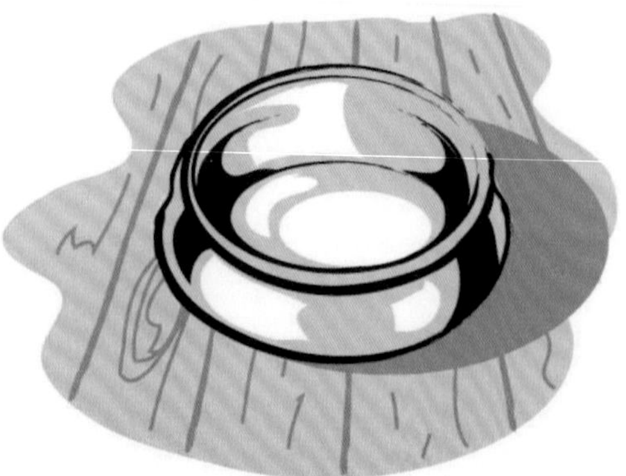

As he spoke he fearlessly patted[13] the head he had recently beaten so hard. Although Buck's hair stood up on end, he did not protest[14]. When the man brought him water, he drank quickly, and later ate a generous meal of raw meat[15], piece by piece from the man's hand.

He was beaten[16] (he knew that), but he was not broken. He saw that he stood no chance against[17] the man with the club. He had learned the lesson, and for the rest of his life he never forgot it. It was his introduction into the world of primitive law.

As the days went by, other dogs came in, some quietly and some raging and roaring like he had. And one by one he watched them being tamed[18] by the man in the red sweater. Buck understood that a man with a club was a law-giver[19], a master to be obeyed[20], though not necessarily a friend.

BUCK'S FEELINGS

- How does Buck feel now?
- How have his feelings changed?
- What do you imagine will happen to him next?

1 strike [straɪk] (v.) 打（動詞三態：strike; struck; struck/stricken）
2 bark [bɑrk] (n.) 吠聲
3 scream [skrim] (n.) 尖叫
4 club [klʌb] (v.) 用棍棒打
5 smash [smæʃ] (v.) 擊潰
6 deliberately [dɪˋlɪbərɪtlɪ] (adv.) 不慌不忙地
7 agony [ˋægənɪ] (n.) 極度痛苦
8 roar [ror] (n.) 吼叫
9 jaw [dʒɔ] (n.) 顎；下巴
10 crash [kræʃ] (v.) 碰撞
11 blow [blo] (n.) 毆打
12 senses [ˋsɛnsɪs] (n.)〔複〕知覺
13 pat [pæt] (v.) 輕拍
14 protest [prəˋtɛst] (v.) 反對
15 raw meat [rɔ mit] 生肉
16 beat [bit] (v.) 打（動詞三態：beat; beat; beat/beaten）
17 stand no chance against 對……沒有勝算
18 tame [tem] (v.) 馴化
19 law-giver [ˋlɔˏgɪvɚ] (n.) 立法者
20 obey [əˋbe] (a.) 遵守

9

Now and again, strangers came to talk to the fat man. They gave him money and took away one of the dogs. Buck wondered where they went, for they never came back. He was frightened of the future. In the end a small man called Perrault paid three hundred dollars for him, and he was led away with Curly, a good-natured[1] Newfoundland dog.

The two dogs were put onto a ship where they were looked after[2] by Perrault and another French-Canadian called François. They were a new kind of man to Buck, and while he developed[3] no affection[4] for them, he grew to respect[5] them. He quickly learnt that they were fair[6] men and too clever about the ways of dogs to be fooled[7] by them. There were also two other dogs on the ship – a large, snow-white dog called Spitz who was quite difficult, and stole Buck's food, and a gloomy[8], quiet dog called Dave who wasn't interested in anything.

As the ship moved northwards the weather grew steadily[9] colder. Eventually[10] the ship stopped, and François tied the dogs together and brought them onto the deck[11]. At the first step upon the cold surface[12], Buck's feet sank[13] into something that was white and soft like mud[14]. He jumped back with a bark. More of this white stuff[15] was falling through the air. He shook[16] himself, but more of it fell upon him.

He sniffed[17] it curiously, then licked some up with his tongue. It was like fire, and the next instant[18] it was gone. This puzzled[19] him. He tried it again, with the same result[20]. The people watching him laughed loudly, and he felt ashamed[21], though he didn't know why, for it was his first snow.

1 good-natured [ˋgudˋnetʃɚd] (a.) 溫厚的
2 look after 照顧
3 develop [dɪˋvɛləp] (v.) 發展
4 affection [əˋfɛkʃən] (n.) 感情
5 respect [rɪˋspɛkt] (v.) 尊重；尊敬
6 fair [fɛr] (a.) 公正的；誠實的
7 fool [ful] (v.) 愚弄
8 gloomy [ˋglumɪ] (a.) 陰鬱的
9 steadily [ˋstɛdəlɪ] (adv.) 穩定地
10 eventually [ɪˋvɛntʃuəlɪ] (n.) 最後地
11 deck [dɛk] (n.) 甲板
12 surface [ˋsɝfɪs] (n.) 表面
13 sink [sɪŋk] (v.) 下沈（動詞三態：sink; sank/sunk; sunk/sunken）
14 mud [mʌd] (n.) 泥
15 stuff [stʌf] (n.) 東西；玩意
16 shake [ʃek] (v.) 抖動（動詞三態：shake; shook; shaken）
17 sniff [snɪf] (v.) 嗅；聞
18 instant [ˋɪnstənt] (n.) 一剎那
19 puzzle [ˋpʌzḷ] (v.) 困惑
20 result [rɪˋzʌlt] (n.) 結果
21 ashamed [əˋʃemd] (a.) 難為情的

THE LAW OF CLUB AND TOOTH

10

Buck's first day on the beach was like a nightmare[1]. Every hour was filled with shock or surprise. He had been suddenly[2] removed[3] from civilization[4] and thrown[5] into the heart of a primitive world. Here there was neither peace nor rest, nor a moment's safety. It was essential[6] to be constantly[7] alert[8], for these dogs and men were not town dogs and men. They were savages[9], all of them, who knew no law but the law of club and tooth.

He had never seen dogs fight like these, and his first experience taught him an unforgettable lesson. He was fortunate that it was Curly who was the victim[10], not himself. Curly, in her friendly way, tried to make friends with a husky dog. The dog was the size of a full-grown wolf, but not half as large as Curly was. There was no warning: only a fast jump, a metallic[11] cut of teeth, and a jump back. Curly's face was ripped[12] open from eye to mouth.

It was wolf fighting, to strike and jump away, but there was more to it than this. Thirty or forty huskies ran to watch. They surrounded[13] the fighters in a silent, watching circle, all licking their lips. Curly rushed at the husky, who struck again and jumped away. He met her next rush with his chest in a strange way that knocked her over. She never got up again. This was what the watching huskies had waited for. They closed in on her, snarling[14] and yelping[15]. Curly was buried, screaming in pain, under the dogs' bodies.

1 nightmare [ˋnaɪt͵mɛr] (n.) 惡夢
2 suddenly [ˋsʌdn̩lɪ] (adv.) 突然地
3 remove [rɪˋmuv] (v.) 遷移
4 civilization [͵sɪvl̩əˋzeʃən] (n.) 文明世界
5 throw [θro] (v.) 丟；投（動詞三態：throw; threw; thrown）
6 essential [ɪˋsɛnʃəl] (a.) 必要的
7 constantly [ˋkɑnstəntlɪ] (adv.) 不斷地
8 alert [əˋlɝt] (a.) 警覺的

It was so sudden and unexpected that Buck was surprised. He saw Spitz watching, laughing. François jumped into the middle of the dogs, helped by three men with clubs and the dogs soon ran away. But Curly lay lifeless in the bloody snow. This scene often came back to Buck. This was the way of his new world. No fair play. Once you were down, that was the end. He would be careful not to go down. Spitz laughed again, and from that moment Buck hated him.

FAIR PLAY

- What does Buck mean by 'fair play'?
- How would you react in such a strange and violent world?

Buck soon received another shock. François fastened[16] him into a harness[17]. He had seen them before on horses when they were working. And he was set to work, pulling François on a sled to the forest around the valley, returning with firewood[18]. He didn't like it, but he was too clever to rebel[19]; he did his best although it was all new and strange. The other dogs – Spitz, the leader, and Dave, nearest the sled – with François and his whip[20], soon taught Buck how to behave when pulling the sled.

9 savage [ˋsævɪdʒ] (n.) 野蠻者
10 victim [ˋvɪktɪm] (n.) 受害者
11 metallic [məˋtælɪk] (a.) 金屬似的
12 rip [rɪp] (v.) 撕；劃破
13 surround [səˋraʊnd] (v.) 圍繞
14 snarl [snɑrl̩] (v.) 吠；嗥
15 yelp [jɛlp] (v.) 吠
16 fasten [ˋfæsn̩] (v.) 紮牢；繫緊
17 harness [ˋhɑrnɪs] (n.) 馬具；挽具
18 firewood [ˋfaɪr,wʊd] (n.) 木柴
19 rebel [rɪˋbɛl] (v.) 反抗
20 whip [hwɪp] (n.) 鞭子

12

Perrault brought three more dogs to make up[1] the team of six to pull the sled. Two brother huskies called Billie and Joe, and an old husky who was blind in one eye called Sol-leks, which means 'angry one'. Spitz attacked[2] the new dogs, and beat Billie, but not Joe. Sol-leks' only ambition[3], like Dave's, was to be left alone. Although, as Buck was to learn later, each of them had another and even more vital[4] ambition.

That night Buck faced the problem of sleeping. He tried to sleep in the tent[5], but Perrault and François threw things and shouted at him until he ran away. A cold wind was blowing. He lay down on the snow but the frost[6] soon made him stand up. He walked around the camp[7], but one place was as cold as another. He went back to see what his team-mates were doing. To his great astonishment[8], they had disappeared.

1 make up 組成
2 attack [əˋtæk] (v.) 攻擊
3 ambition [æmˋbɪʃən] (n.) 雄心
4 vital [ˋvaɪtl̩] (a.) 生死攸關的
5 tent [tɛnt] (n.) 帳篷
6 frost [frɑst] (n.) 霜；嚴寒
7 camp [kæmp] (n.) 營地
8 astonishment [əˋstɑnɪʃmənt] (n.) 錯愕

He wandered around unhappily, looking for them. Suddenly, as he walked round the tent, the snow gave way[9] under his front feet and there was Billie curled up[10] under the snow like a warm ball. It was another lesson. Buck selected[11] a spot[12], and dug[13] a hole for himself. In a moment, the heat from his body filled the small space and he was soon asleep.

Buck didn't wake up until he heard the noises of the waking camp. At first he didn't remember where he was. It had snowed in the night and he was completely buried. He was frightened and thought perhaps he was in a trap[14]. But then he jumped straight up into the bright light of day. He saw the camp in front of him and he knew where he was. Everything came back to him from the walk with Manuel, to the hole he had dug for himself the night before.

9 give way 使瓦解
10 curl up 蜷曲
11 select [səˋlɛkt] (v.) 選擇
12 spot [spɑt] (n.) 地點
13 dig [dɪg] (v.) 挖掘（動詞三態：dig; dug; dug）
14 trap [træp] (n.) 陷阱

14 When François saw Buck he shouted to Perrault: 'What did I say? Buck certainly learns quickly.'

Perrault nodded[1] seriously. He was a courier[2] for the Canadian Government, carrying important letters, and he was anxious[3] to get the best dogs. He was particularly pleased about owning Buck.

Three more huskies were added to the team, making nine dogs, and soon they were in harness and moving up the trail[4]. Buck was glad to be moving. Though the work was hard, he didn't dislike it. He was surprised at the eagerness[5] of the whole team, and even more surprised at Dave and Sol-leks, who were completely changed by the harness. They were no longer passive[6] and uninterested[7]. Now they were alert and active. Pulling the sled seemed to be what they lived for and the only thing that they enjoyed.

Dave was nearest the sled, Buck was in front of him, then came Sol-leks; the rest of the team was ahead in single file up to the leader, Spitz. They had placed Buck between Sol-leks and Dave on purpose[8], so that he could learn what to do. He was a good learner and they were good teachers, helping him to learn with their sharp teeth. But by the end of the day he had mastered his work and François' whip hit him less often.

1 nod [nɑd] (v.) 點頭
2 courier [ˋkʊrɪɚ] (n.) 快遞信差
3 anxious [ˋæŋkʃəs] (a.) 渴望的
4 trail [trel] (n.) 小道
5 eagerness [ˋigɚnɪs] (n.) 渴望；熱切
6 passive [ˋpæsɪv] (a.) 消極的
7 uninterested [ʌnˋɪntərɪstɪd] (a.) 興趣缺缺的
8 on purpose 故意地
9 canyon [ˋkænjən] (n.) 峽谷
10 timber line 森林帶的界線

It was a hard day's run up the canyon[9]. They passed the timber line[10], they crossed glaciers[11] and snowdrifts[12] hundreds of meters deep, and they went over the great Chilcoot Divide[13], which guards the sad, lonely north.

They traveled quickly past a chain of lakes, and late that night they pulled into a large camp at the head of Lake Bennet. There were thousands of gold-seekers waiting there for the ice to melt in spring. Buck made his hole in the snow and slept, exhausted[14].

Day after day Buck worked hard in the harness. The team started off[15] in the dark and then stopped to camp in the dark, eating their bit of fish, and crawling to sleep in the snow. Buck was very hungry. The kilo of dried salmon, which was what the dogs got each day, was never enough for him. The other dogs weighed less and were used to this way of life, so they managed to[16] keep in good condition.

He found, however, that the ones who finished their food quickly, would steal his. To stop this, he ate as fast as they did. He was so hungry that he even took what didn't belong to him. He saw Pike, one of the new dogs, steal a piece of bacon when Perrault's back was turned. He did the same thing the following day, getting away with the whole piece. The men were very angry, but did not suspect[17] him, and another new dog, Dub, was punished[18] for it.

Theft was one of the things Buck had to learn to survive in his new hostile[19] Northland environment. He knew he had to change to fit[20] into these harsh new conditions, or face a quick and terrible death.

11 glacier [ˋgleʃɚ] (n.) 冰河
12 snowdrift [ˋsno͵drɪft] (n.)（為風所吹集的）雪堆
13 divide [dəˋvaɪd] (n.) 分水嶺
14 exhausted [ɪgˋzɔstɪd] (a.) 精疲力竭的
15 start off 出發
16 manage to 設法做到
17 suspect [səˋspɛkt] (v.) 懷疑
18 punish [ˋpʌnɪʃ] (v.) 懲罰
19 hostile [ˋhɑstɪl] (a.) 不友善的
20 fit [fɪt] (v.) 適合

BUCK'S NEW LIFE

- What is Buck's new life like?
- How is it different from his old life?
- What lessons has he learned to help him survive?

His development was fast. His muscles became hard as iron. He could eat anything. His sight and sense of smell became very sharp, while his hearing developed so much that in his sleep he knew whether the smallest sound meant danger or not. He learned to bite the ice out when it collected between his toes. When he was thirsty and there was a thick layer[1] of ice over the water hole, he would break it by dropping onto it with his front legs. He also learnt to smell the wind and decide what would happen in the night, so that he always made his sleeping hole in the most sheltered[2] place.

Not only did he learn by experience, but long-dead instincts rose[3] in him again. The years of domesticated[4] dog generations[5] fell from him. It wasn't difficult for him to learn to fight like wolves, because that was how his ancestors[6] had fought. And when, on still cold nights, he pointed his nose at a star and howled[7] long and wolf-like, it was as if his ancestors were howling through him.

1 layer [ˋleɚ] (n.) 層
2 sheltered [ˋʃɛltɚd] (a.) 掩蔽的
3 rise [raɪz] (v.) 上升（動詞三態：rise; rose; risen）
4 domesticated [dəˋmɛstə͵ketɪd] (a.) 被馴養了的
5 generation [͵dʒɛnəˋreʃən] (n.) 世代
6 ancestor [ˋænsɛstɚ] (n.) 祖先
7 howl [haʊl] (v.) 嗥叫
8 conditions [kənˋdɪʃənz] (n.)〔複〕環境
9 cunning [ˋkʌnɪŋ] (a.) 狡猾的
10 provoke [prəˋvok] (v.) 挑釁；激怒
11 miserable [ˋmɪzərəb!] (a.) 悽慘的
12 occupy [ˋɑkjə͵paɪ] (v.) 佔領
13 avoid [əˋvɔɪd] (v.) 避免
14 enemy [ˋɛnəmɪ] (n.) 敵人

THE PRIMITIVE BEAST

17 The primitive beast was strong inside Buck. It grew stronger under the difficult conditions[8] of working life. But it was a secret growth. His new cunning[9] gave him self-control. He didn't fight and did nothing to provoke[10] Spitz.

However, Spitz never lost an opportunity to try and start a fight with Buck. A fight between them could only end in the death of one or the other. One night they made a miserable[11] camp on Lake Le Barge. Heavy snow, a wind that cut like a knife and darkness forced them to try and find a camping place even though they were surrounded by high walls of rock. Perrault and François had to make their fire and put their sleeping blankets on the ice of the lake itself.

Buck made his sleeping hole under a sheltering rock. It was so comfortable and warm that he didn't really want to leave it but he went to eat. When he returned, he found it occupied[12] by Spitz. Till now Buck had avoided[13] trouble with his enemy[14], but this was too much. He jumped on Spitz with a strength and anger that surprised them both.

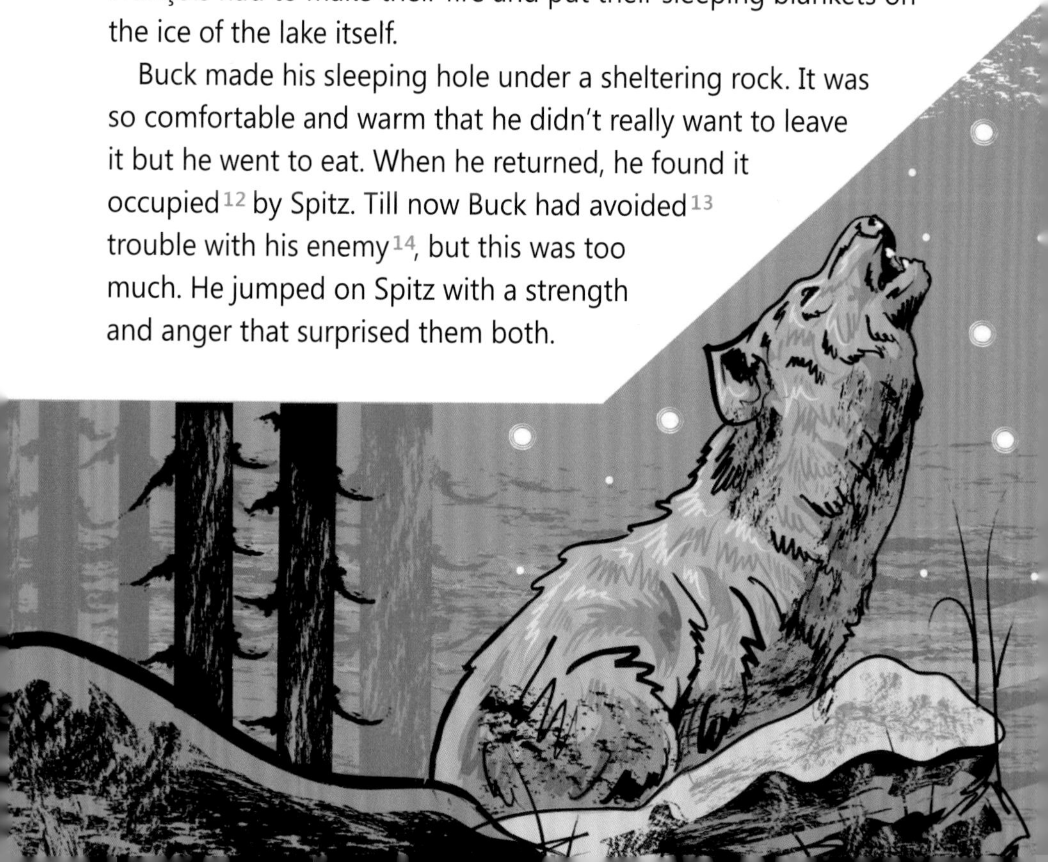

18 The two dogs circled[1] each other, looking for the right moment to attack. But it was then that the unexpected happened. The camp was suddenly full of starving[2] huskies from an Indian village, who had smelt food. They had crept in while Buck and Spitz were fighting. François and Perrault jumped in among them with their clubs but the dogs showed their teeth and fought back. They had been made mad by the smell of food. A food box fell over and immediately twenty dogs were fighting for bread and bacon. The men clubbed them; the dogs howled as they were hit, but still they kept eating until nothing was left.

Buck had never seen such dogs. They looked like skeletons[3] covered in thin skin, but with fiery[4] eyes and teeth showing. Their hunger-madness made them terrifying[5]. Buck was attacked by three huskies, and in a moment his head and shoulders were ripped and slashed[6]. As Buck attacked another husky, he felt teeth bite into his throat. It was Spitz, attacking him from the side.

1 circle [ˋsɝkl̩] (v.) 繞行
2 starving [ˋstɑrvɪŋ] (a.) 極饑餓的
3 skeleton [ˋskɛlətn̩] (n.) 骷髏
4 fiery [ˋfaɪərɪ] (a.) 火一般的
5 terrifying [ˋtɛrə͵faɪɪŋ] (a.) 令人害怕的
6 slash [slæʃ] (v.) 猛擊

19 Perrault and François ran to help him. The wild, starving dogs moved away, and Buck shook himself free. Billie ran through the savage dogs and off across the ice, followed by Pike and Dub, with the rest of the team behind. As Buck got ready to follow them, Spitz attacked him again; he knew that if he fell, the huskies would kill him. He waited for Spitz's charge[7], then ran off after the rest of the team.

The nine team-dogs found shelter[8] in the forest. All of them were wounded[9] in several places. At daybreak[10] they limped[11] back to the camp, to find the invaders[12] gone and Perrault and François angry. Half of their food supply[13] was gone. Nothing was left untouched. François stopped checking the equipment[14] to care for the wounded dogs.

7 charge [tʃɑrdʒ] (n.) 攻擊
8 shelter [`ʃɛltɚ] (n.) 掩蔽處
9 wounded [`wundɪd] (a.) 受傷的
10 daybreak [`de͵brek] (n.) 黎明
11 limp [lɪmp] (v.) 一瘸一拐地走
12 invader [ɪn`vedɚ] (n.) 入侵者
13 supply [sə`plaɪ] (n.) 供應品
14 equipment [ɪ`kwɪpmənt] (n.) 設備

20 With six hundred kilometers still to Dawson, Perrault was anxious to get started. Now the wounded team had to struggle[1] painfully[2] over the hardest part of the trail – The Thirty Mile River. The river was flowing[3] and the only ice for them to walk on was in quiet places near the bank. Six days of exhausting walking were needed to cover the distance[4], and at every step there was the risk of death to dog and man.

A dozen times Perrault, who was still in front, fell through the ice of the river. He was saved only by the pole[5] he held crossways[6] over his body. It was very cold, with temperatures[7] of minus[8] fifty. Every time he fell through the ice, they had to stop so he could build a fire and dry his clothes or risk dying.

Nothing stopped Perrault – that is why he was a government courier. Every day he took many risks. Once the sled broke through the ice with Dave and Buck. They were half-frozen and almost drowned by the time they were dragged[9] out. They were made to run round a fire, sweating and thawing[10], to save their lives.

Another time, Spitz went through, dragging the whole team after him as far as Buck, who pulled back with Dave and François to stop the sled going in. On another occasion, the ice cracked[11] before and behind, and the only way to get out was up the rocky cliff[12] face. The dogs were pulled up one by one on a long rope. They then had to look for somewhere to get back down. That day, they only traveled a few hundred meters along the river.

1 struggle [ˋstrʌgl̩] (v.) 艱難地行進
2 painfully [ˋpenfəlɪ] (adv.) 痛苦地
3 flow [flo] (v.) 流動
4 distance [ˋdɪstəns] (n.) 距離
5 pole [pol] (n.) 竿子
6 crossways [ˋkrɔs͵wez] (adv.) 交叉地
7 temperature [ˋtɛmprətʃɚ] (n.) 溫度
8 minus [ˋmaɪnəs] (a.) 零下的

PERRAULT AND FRANÇOIS

- What type of men are Perrault and François? With a partner think of three adjectives to describe them.

By the time they reached the Teslin River and good ice, Buck and the other dogs were exhausted. Perrault, to make up lost time, pushed them hard. The first day they covered fifty kilometers to Big Salmon; the next day fifty more to Little Salmon; and the third day sixty kilometers, which brought them very close to the Five Fingers.

Buck's feet were not as hard as the huskies' feet and all day long he limped in pain. Once camp was made he lay down like a dead dog, and even though he was hungry, he wouldn't move to receive his food. So François had to bring it to him. He also rubbed[13] Buck's feet for half an hour each night, and used the tops of his own boots to make four shoes for Buck, which was a great relief[14].

Buck made the two men laugh one morning when François forgot to put the shoes on. He lay on his back waving his feet in the air, and refused[15] to move until they had been put on. Later his feet grew hard, and the worn-out[16] shoes were thrown away.

9 drag [dræg] (v.) 拖
10 thaw [θɔ] (v.) 融化；解凍
11 crack [kræk] (v.) 爆裂
12 cliff [klɪf] (n.) 懸崖；峭壁
13 rub [rʌb] (v.) 摩擦
14 relief [rɪ`lif] (n.) 緩和；減輕
15 refuse [rɪ`fjuz] (v.) 不肯
16 worn-out [`worn`aʊt] (a.) 穿破的

22 At the Pelly one morning as they were harnessing[1] up, Dolly, who had always been quiet, went mad. She made a long wolf howl that put fear into the heart of the dogs, and jumped straight at Buck. He had never seen a dog go mad. He was so afraid he ran, with Dolly chasing[2] just behind. When François whistled he came racing back, gasping[3] for breath. As Buck rushed past him, François brought an axe down on mad Dolly's head and killed her.

Buck crawled over to the sled and lay exhausted and helpless. This was Spitz's opportunity[4]. He jumped on Buck and bit him twice. Then he ripped and tore Buck's flesh[5] to the bone. But then François' whip came down, and Buck had the satisfaction of seeing Spitz receive the worst beating given to one of the team so far.

'That Spitz is a real devil,' remarked[6] Perrault. 'Some day he'll kill Buck.'

'Buck is two devils,' was François' answer. 'I've been watching and I know for sure. Listen: one day he'll get angry and he'll chew[7] Spitz up and spit[8] him out on the snow.'

BUCK AND SPITZ

- With a partner discuss the relationship between Buck and Spitz. Why does Spitz hate Buck so much?
- What does François mean when he says: 'he'll chew Spitz up and spit him out on the snow'?

From then on it was war between the two dogs. Spitz, as leader of the team, felt threatened[9] by this strange Southland dog. He had known many Southland dogs, but they were all too soft, and had died from the work, the cold or of hunger. Buck was the exception[10]. He was as strong, savage and cunning as the huskies. He could wait, with a patience[11] that was absolutely[12] primitive.

Buck wanted the fight for leadership to happen because it was his nature, and because he felt the pride[13] of the trail dog now. He openly and deliberately threatened Spitz's leadership.

1 harness [ˋhɑrnɪs] (v.) 上挽具
2 chase [tʃes] (v.) 追逐
3 gasp [gæsp] (v.) 上氣不接下氣
4 opportunity [ˏɑpɚˋtjunətɪ] (n.) 機會
5 flesh [flɛʃ] (n.) 肉；肌肉
6 remark [rɪˋmɑrk] (v.) 評論
7 chew [tʃu] (v.) 咀嚼
8 spit [spɪt] (v.) 吐
9 threatened [ˋθrɛtn̩d] (a.) 受到威脅的
10 exception [ɪkˋsɛpʃən] (n.) 例外
11 patience [ˋpeʃəns] (n.) 耐性
12 absolutely [ˋæbsəˏlutlɪ] (adv.) 絕對地
13 pride [praɪd] (n.) 驕傲

24

Once Pike did not appear for harnessing so Spitz went searching[1] for him, and was about to attack when Buck got in the way. He attacked Spitz, knocking him over, so that Pike could attack him. Buck joined in, too. But François came and whipped Buck until he stopped.

As Dawson grew closer, Buck continued to get between Spitz and those he wanted to punish, but he did it craftily[2], when François was not around. Because of this, all the other dogs started behaving badly, except Dave and Sol-leks. There were continual problems between the two dogs. François knew that sooner or later the life-and-death struggle for the position[3] of the leader would occur[4].

But there was no opportunity, and as they pulled into Dawson, the great fight was still to come. In Dawson, there were many men and countless[5] dogs. Buck saw them all at work. It seemed normal that dogs should work, doing all the pulling jobs which horses did in California. Every night, regularly[6] at nine, at twelve, at three, the huskies howled a nocturnal[7] song, a weird[8] chant[9], which Buck joined in with. It was an old song, old as the breed[10] itself – one of the first songs of an ancient[11] world in a time when songs were sad.

25 Seven days later, they dropped down onto the Yukon Trail, and started back to Dyea and Salt Water. Perrault was carrying letters which were even more urgent[12] than those he had brought in. He wanted to make this the fastest trip of the year. Several things helped him. The week's rest had given the dogs time to get back to normal health. The trail which they had taken on the way to Dawson was now packed hard because of later travelers. And the police had arranged for deposits[13] of food to be left in two or three places, for dog and man, so he was travelling light.

They did a good seventy-five kilometer run on the first day. And on the second dashed[14] up the Yukon, well on their way to Pelly. But this speed was hard work for François, because the revolt[15] led by Buck had destroyed[16] the unity of the team. All the dogs now showed disrespect to Spitz, stealing his food and attacking him.

1 search [sɝtʃ] (v.) 尋找
2 craftily [ˋkræftɪlɪ] (adv.) 狡猾地
3 position [pəˋzɪʃən] (n.) 位置；職位
4 occur [əˋkɝ] (v.) 發生
5 countless [ˋkaʊntlɪs] (a.) 數不盡的
6 regularly [ˋrɛgjələlɪ] (adv.) 經常地
7 nocturnal [nɑkˋtɝnl̩] (a.) 夜間發生的
8 weird [wɪrd] (a.) 神祕的
9 chant [tʃænt] (n.) 歌；曲子
10 breed [brid] (n.) 品種
11 ancient [ˋenʃənt] (a.) 古老的
12 urgent [ˋɝdʒənt] (a.) 緊急的
13 deposit [dɪˋpɑzɪt] (n.) 放置
14 dash [dæʃ] (v.) 急奔
15 revolt [rɪˋvolt] (n.) 反叛
16 destroy [dɪˋstrɔɪ] (v.) 破壞

26 The relationship between the other dogs had also changed, and, apart from[1] Dave and Sol-leks, they often fought each other. François knew that Buck was behind all the trouble, and Buck knew that he knew. But Buck was too clever to let him catch him again. He worked well in the harness, because he enjoyed the work, but it was a great delight[2] to him to slyly[3] make the others fight amongst themselves.

At the mouth of the Tahkeena, one night after dinner, Dub found a rabbit, but couldn't quite catch it. In a second the whole team was chasing it. A hundred meters away, there was another camp with fifty huskies. These dogs also joined the chase. The rabbit sped[4] down the river, and up a valley. It ran lightly on the surface of the snow while the dogs ploughed[5] through it using their strength. Buck was leading the pack[6], but he couldn't catch the rabbit. He felt his instincts rise in him as he chased. He was at the head of the pack, running after a wild thing – living meat. He wanted to kill it with his own teeth and wash his nose in its warm blood. He was consumed[7] by feelings deep within him, going back to the beginning of time.

But Spitz was as cold and calculating[8] as usual. He ran away from the pack and cut across a narrow piece of land while Buck and the others followed the rabbit and the river around a U-shaped bend[9]. Buck did not realize this. As Buck rounded[10] the bend he suddenly saw Spitz jump down in front of the rabbit. The rabbit could not turn, and as the dog's teeth broke its back, it shrieked[11] loudly. Hearing the noise, the full pack behind Buck showed their delight.

1 apart from 除……之外
2 delight [dɪˋlaɪt] (n.) 樂趣
3 slyly [ˋslaɪlɪ] (adv.) 狡猾地
4 speed [spid] (v.) 迅速前進（動詞三態：speed; sped / speeded; sped / speeded)
5 plough [plaʊ] (v.) 開路
6 pack [pæk] (n.) 一群
7 consume [kənˋsjum] (v.) 吞噬
8 calculate [ˋkælkjə͵let] (v.) 計算；估計
9 bend [bɛnd] (n.) 轉彎
10 round [raʊnd] (v.) 環繞而行
11 shriek [ʃrik] (v.) 尖叫

27

Buck did not cry out. He did not slow down, but ran into Spitz, shoulder to shoulder. The dogs rolled over in the powdery[1] snow. Spitz got up immediately, and slashed Buck's shoulder, then jumped clear.

Buck knew the time had come. They circled around each other, snarling and watching for an advantage[2]. The huskies were now in an expectant[3] circle, and everything was silent. But there was nothing new or strange in this. It was what had always been, the way of things.

Spitz was a practiced[4] fighter. From Spitzbergen through the Arctic, and across Canada, he had fought all kinds of dogs and achieved[5] mastery[6] over them. His rage was bitter, but never blind. In his passion to break and destroy, he never forgot that his enemy had the same passion[7] to break and destroy. He never rushed till he was prepared to receive a rush[8]; never attacked until he had first defended an attack.

1 powdery [ˋpaudərɪ] (a.) 粉狀的
2 advantage [ədˋvæntɪdʒ] (n.) 優勢
3 expectant [ɪkˋspɛktənt] (a.) 期待的
4 practiced [ˋpræktɪst] (a.) 熟練的
5 achieve [əˋtʃiv] (v.) 到達
6 mastery [ˋmæstərɪ] (n.) 支配；統治

28

In vain[9] Buck tried to sink his teeth into the neck of the big white dog. Wherever his teeth bit to find softer meat, Spitz's teeth blocked[10] him. Tooth clashed[11] with tooth, and lips were cut and bleeding[12], but Buck could not break through Spitz's guard. Then he tried a series of rushes at Spitz, going for the dog's throat, and each time Spitz slashed him and got away. He tried rushing, as if it were for the throat, then suddenly pulling back his head, and trying to knock him over with his shoulder. But each time Buck's shoulder was slashed as Spitz jumped away.

Spitz was untouched, while Buck was streaming[13] with blood and panting[14] loudly. The fight was growing desperate[15]. And all the time the silent wolfish circle waited to finish off[16] whichever dog went down.

7 passion [ˋpæʃən] (n.) 激情
8 rush [rʌʃ] (v.) (n.) 猛攻
9 in vain 徒勞無功
10 block [blɑk] (v.) 阻擋
11 clash [klæʃ] (v.) 砰地碰撞
12 bleed [blid] (v.) 流血（動詞三態：bleed; bled; bled）
13 stream [strim] (v.) 流
14 pant [pænt] (v.) 氣喘
15 desperate [ˋdɛspərɪt] (a.) 情急拼命的
16 finish off 毀滅

29

But Buck possessed[1] a quality that made for greatness – imagination. He fought by instinct, but he could also fight with his head. He rushed as though trying the old shoulder trick, but at the last moment dived[2] down close to the snow. His teeth closed on Spitz's left front leg. There was a crunch[3] of breaking bone, and the white dog faced him on three legs. Three times Buck tried to knock him over, then repeated the trick and broke Spitz's right front leg. Despite[4] his pain and helplessness, Spitz tried to get up. But he saw the silent circle closing in upon him.

There was no hope for him. Buck moved for the final rush. The circle was so close he could feel the breaths of the huskies on his back. Then Buck jumped; shoulder met shoulder and Spitz went down. The circle became a dot[5] on the moonlit[6] snow, and Spitz disappeared from view. Buck stood and looked on, the successful champion[7], the primitive beast who had made his kill and found it good.

THE FIGHT

- Describe the fight in your own words.
- How does Buck win the fight?
- Why is he called 'the primitive beast'?

1 possess [pə`zɛs] (v.) 擁有
2 dive [daɪv] (v.) 潛入
3 crunch [krʌntʃ] (n.) 嘎吱作響地咬嚼
4 despite [dɪ`spaɪt] (prep.) 儘管
5 dot [dɑt] (n.) 小圓點
6 moonlit [`munlɪt] (a.) 月光照耀的
7 champion [`tʃæmpɪən] (n.) 冠軍

BECOMING THE LEADER

'What did I say? I was right when I said that Buck was two devils.'

This is what François said next morning when he discovered Spitz missing and Buck covered with wounds. He pulled him to the fire and pointed them out.

'That Spitz fought like hell[1],' said Perrault when he saw the rips[2] and cuts.

'And Buck fought like two hells,' was François' answer. 'And now we'll make good time. No more Spitz, no more trouble.'

SPITZ

- Are the men sorry that Spitz is dead? Why/Why not?
- Do you think they expected the fight?

The dog-driver harnessed the dogs and Buck trotted[3] up to the place Spitz would have occupied as leader. François didn't notice him and brought Sol-leks to the desired[4] position. In his judgment Sol-leks was the best lead-dog left. Buck jumped on Sol-leks in anger, driving him back and standing in his place.

'Look at Buck,' François cried. 'He killed Spitz and thinks he can take his job. Go away!'

1 like hell 拼命地
2 rip [rɪp] (n.) 裂口
3 trot [trɑt] (v.) 小跑；快步
4 desired [dɪ`zaɪrd] (a.) 想要的
5 fix sb 修理某人
6 scratch [skrætʃ] (v.) 搔
7 shrug [ʃrʌg] (v.) 聳肩
8 sign [saɪn] (n.) 表示；手勢

31 But Buck refused to move. François took Buck by the back of his neck and pulled him to the side and put Sol-leks back. The old dog did not like it and showed he was afraid of Buck, and as soon as François turned his back Buck again pushed Sol-leks out.

François was angry. 'Now, by God, I'll fix you[5]!' he shouted, coming back with a heavy club in his hand.

Buck remembered the man in the red sweater and moved back, snarling with rage. The driver got on with his work, and called Buck later to put him in his old place in front of Dave. Buck moved back two or three steps. François followed him, and again Buck moved backwards. François threw down his club, thinking Buck was afraid of being beaten. But Buck was in open revolt. He wanted the leadership. It was his by right. He had earned it.

Perrault came and for an hour they tried to catch Buck. He didn't run away, but always kept just out of reach. Perrault was angry – they should have left an hour ago. François scratched[6] his head, and the courier shrugged[7] his shoulders in a sign[8] that they were beaten. Then François went over to Sol-leks and called to Buck. Buck laughed, as dogs laugh, but kept his distance. François put Sol-leks back in his old place. François called again but still Buck laughed and didn't come.

'Throw down your club,' said Perrault.

32

François did, and Buck trotted in, laughing triumphantly[1] and took up the position at the head of the team. His harness was fastened, and they started out on the river trail.

François had always thought that Buck was good, but he had never realized[2] how good until now. Immediately Buck took up the duties of leadership. Where judgment[3] and quick thinking were needed, he showed himself superior even to Spitz. But it was in giving the law and making his mates live up to[4] it that Buck was best. He made the lazy Pike pull better, he punished Joe – a thing Spitz had never managed to do, and the team was immediately better. At Rink Rapids[5] two native huskies, Teek and Koona, were added, and the speed with which Buck made them fit amazed[6] François.

'There was never a dog like Buck!' he cried. 'He's worth a thousand dollars, by God! What do you say, Perrault?'

And Perrault nodded. He was ahead of the record time, and increasing it daily. The trail was in excellent condition, well-packed and hard, and there was no new snow. The temperature dropped to minus 50 and stayed there for the whole trip.

LEADERSHIP

- What do François and Perrault think about Buck? Why is this?
- What qualities do you need to be a good leader? With a partner discuss someone you think is a good leader.

1 triumphantly [traɪˋʌmfəntlɪ] (adv.) 得意洋洋地
2 realize [ˋrɪəˏlaɪz] (v.) 了解到
3 judgment [ˋdʒʌdʒmənt] (n.) 判斷力
4 live up to 實踐
5 rapids [ˋræpɪdz] (n.)〔複〕急流
6 amaze [əˋmez] (v.) 使吃驚
7 run [rʌn] (n.) 路程
8 section [ˋsɛkʃən] (n.) 地段
9 slope [slop] (n.) 坡度
10 averaged [ˋævərɪdʒɪd] (a.) 平均的
11 admiration [ˏædməˋreʃən] (n.) 欽佩
12 weep [wip] (v.) 哭泣

The Thirty Mile River was covered with a layer of ice, and in one day they traveled the same distance that had taken ten days on the way there. In one run[7] they made the ninety kilometer section[8] from the foot of Lake Le Barge to the White Horse Rapids. And on the last night of the second week they topped White Pass and dropped down the sea slope[9] with the lights of Skaguay and the ships below.

It was a record run. Each day for fourteen days they had averaged[10] sixty kilometers.

François and Perrault were heroes for the next three days, and the dog-team was the center of admiration[11]. Then official orders came. François called Buck to him, threw his arms round him and wept[12] over him. And like other men, François and Perrault passed out of Buck's life forever.

A Scotsman took charge of him and his mates[13], and in the company of a dozen other dog-teams they started back over the weary[14] trail to Dawson. It wasn't easy now, but hard work each day with a heavy load[15] behind. This was the mail train, carrying news from the world to the men looking for gold.

Buck did not like it, but he worked hard, taking pride in it like Dave and Sol-leks. He also made sure the team did their fair share of the work. It was a monotonous[16] life. At a certain time the cooks got up, fires were built, and breakfast was eaten. Then they packed up, harnessed the dogs, and were on their way an hour before dawn. At night, camp was made. Some people cut wood for fires, others brought water or ice for the cooks and the dogs were fed with fish, which was their best point in the day. After that they wandered[17] around.

13 mate [met] (n.) 同伴
14 weary [ˋwɪrɪ] (a.) 疲倦的
15 load [lod] (n.) 裝載
16 monotonous [məˋnɑtənəs] (a.) 單調的
17 wander [ˋwɑndɚ] (v.) 漫遊

34

There were more than one hundred dogs altogether, with some fierce[1] fighters amongst them. But three battles with the fiercest brought Buck to mastery, so that they all got out of his way when he showed his teeth.

Best of all, perhaps, Buck loved to lie dreaming near the fire. Sometimes he thought of Judge Miller's big house in the sunny Santa Clara valley, of the swimming tanks[2] and the house dogs. More often, though, he remembered the man in the red sweater, the death of Curly, the great fight with Spitz, and the good things he had eaten or would like to eat.

And sometimes when he lay by the fire his mind would wander back through older lives. He would see himself with a short, hairy man who made strange sounds and was afraid of the dark. The man was almost naked[3], wearing a skin, and his only weapon[4] was a stick[5] with a stone at the end of it. And beyond the firelight, Buck could see the eyes of dangerous animals, and hear the noises they made in the night. They were the sights and sounds of another, earlier world.

BUCK'S DREAMS

- What does Buck dream?
- What is the 'earlier world' that Buck dreams of?
- Who is the 'short, hairy man'?
- Why is this world important to Buck?

1 fierce [fɪrs] (a.) 兇猛的
2 tank [tæŋk] (n.) 槽
3 naked [ˋnekɪd] (a.) 赤裸的
4 weapon [ˋwɛpən] (n.) 武器
5 stick [stɪk] (n.) 棍；棒

35

It was a hard trip, pulling the mail, and the heavy work wore[1] them down. They had lost weight and were in poor condition when they got to Dawson, and needed ten days or a week's rest at least. But in two days' time they dropped down the Yukon bank, loaded with letters for the outside world. The dogs were tired, the drivers grumbling[2], and to make things worse, it snowed every day. This meant a soft trail and heavier pulling for the dogs. But the drivers were fair to the animals through the whole journey.

Each night the dogs were fed first and each driver looked after the feet of the dogs in his team. Still, their strength decreased[3]. Since the beginning of the winter they had dragged sleds two thousand four hundred kilometers. That distance affects[4] even the toughest. Buck stood[5] it, keeping his mates at work and maintaining[6] discipline[7], though he, too, was very tired.

Dave suffered[8] most. The drivers couldn't understand what was wrong; it seemed to be something internal[9]. By the time they had reached Cassiar Bar, he was so weak that he kept falling, and the driver took him out of the harness, and put Sol-leks in his position in front of the sled. He wanted Dave to rest by running free behind the sled. But for Dave this was terrible: he hated the idea of another dog in his position.

36 He managed to keep up with the sleds until they next stopped. Then the driver found Dave standing in front of the sled in his proper[10] place. The drivers discussed this, because they had all known dogs who would rather die doing their work than be prevented[11], however sick they were. So in the end, his driver put his harness back on, and they set off[12] with Dave in his old place. As they traveled, he often fell, or cried out with the pain inside.

The next morning he was too weak to travel, although he crawled towards his old place. But it was the last his mates saw of him. Dave lay gasping in the snow, desperate to be with them. They could hear him howling sadly until they went round the next bend on the trail. Then the train[13] halted[14]. The Scottish driver walked slowly back to the place they had camped. The men stopped talking. A gunshot[15] rang out. The man came back quickly. The whips snapped[16]; the sled bells tinkled[17]; the sleds slid onwards. But Buck knew, and every dog knew, what had happened.

SURVIVAL

- What had happened to Dave? Why?
- Do you think what happened was fair?
- Discuss the phrase 'survival of the fittest'.

1 wear [wɛr] (v.) 削弱（動詞三態：wear; wore; worn）
2 grumble [`grʌmbḷ] (v.) 發牢騷
3 decrease [dɪ`kris] (v.) 減少
4 affect [ə`fɛkt] (v.) 發生作用
5 stand [stænd] (v.) 忍受（動詞三態：stand; stood; stood）
6 maintain [men`ten] (v.) 維持
7 discipline [`dɪsəplɪn] (n.) 紀律
8 suffer [`sʌfɚ] (v.) 受苦
9 internal [ɪn`tɝnḷ] (a.) 體內的
10 proper [`prɑpɚ] (a.) 專有的
11 prevent [prɪ`vɛnt] (v.) 阻止
12 set off 出發；動身
13 train [tren] (n.) 縱隊
14 halt [hɔlt] (v.) 停止
15 gunshot [`gʌn,ʃɑt] (n.) 射擊
16 snap [snæp] (v.) 劈啪作聲
17 tinkle [`tɪŋkḷ] (v.) 叮噹作響

THE TOIL OF TRACE AND TRAIL

37 Thirty days after it left Dawson, the Salt Water Mail, pulled by Buck and his mates, arrived in Skaguay. Buck's eighty kilograms had gone down to seventy. Some dogs were in worse condition. Pike and Sol-leks had hurt their legs and Dub his shoulder. All the dogs' feet hurt. They were dead tired[1] after their prolonged[2] period of very hard work and with good reason. In less than five months they had traveled three thousand seven hundred kilometers.

The drivers expected a long stopover[3]. They themselves had covered one thousand eight hundred kilometers with two days' rest. But so many men had rushed to the Klondike, and so many wives, relations and sweethearts[4] had stayed home, that the mail had turned into mountains. Also there were the official orders. Fresh teams of Hudson Bay dogs were to replace[5] the dogs which were too worn out to continue on the trail. And the latter were to be sold.

On the fourth morning, two men from the States[6] bought Buck and his mates, harness and all. They were called Hal and Charles. Charles was middle-aged, with weak, watery eyes. Hal was about twenty, with a big Colt pistol[7] and a hunting knife on his belt. Both men were clearly out of place, and why people like them had come to the north was a mystery[8]. When Buck and his mates got to their new owners' camp, he saw everything was done badly. Buck saw a woman called Mercedes. She was Charles's wife and Hal's sister. It was a family party.

Buck watched them nervously as they started to take down the tent and load the sled. The tent was rolled up three times larger then it should have been. The tin[9] dishes were packed away unwashed. Mercedes continually moved around, getting in the way of her men, chattering[10] all the time, complaining and offering[11] advice.

1 dead tired 極度疲倦的
2 prolonged [prə`lɔŋd] (a.) 拉長的
3 stopover [`stɑp͵ovɚ] (n.) 中途停留
4 sweetheart [`swit͵hɑrt] (n.) 情人
5 replace [rɪ`ples] (v.) 取代
6 the States 美國
7 pistol [`pɪstḷ] (n.) 手槍
8 mystery [`mɪstərɪ] (n.) 難以理解的事物
9 tin [tɪn] (a.) 錫製的
10 chatter [`tʃætɚ] (v.) 喋喋不休
11 offer [`ɔfɚ] (v.) 提供

BUCK'S NEW OWNERS

- What are Buck's new owners's like?
- If you were Buck, how would you feel about working for these people and why?
- What do you think is going to happen?

Three men came over and watched them, laughing to each other.

'You've got a heavy load,' said one of them, 'If I were you I wouldn't take the tent.'

'Impossible!' cried Mercedes. 'How could I manage without a tent?'

'It's springtime, and you won't get any more cold weather,' the man replied.

She shook her head, and Charles and Hal put the last things on top of the mountainous[1] load.

'Do you think it will be all right?' one of the men asked.

'Why shouldn't it be?' Charles demanded[2], rather annoyed[3].

'It seems a bit top-heavy[4]. That's all,' the man answered quietly.

Charles turned his back and tied the ropes over the load as well as he could.

'And of course the dogs can pull all day with that load behind them,' said another of the men.

'Certainly,' said Hal, and he turned to the dogs. 'Mush[5]!' he shouted. 'Mush on!'

The dogs pulled hard for a few moments, then relaxed. They were unable to move the sled.

'The lazy creatures[6]! I'll show them!' Hal shouted, preparing to whip the dogs.

But Mercedes stopped him, crying, 'Oh, Hal, you mustn't!' She took the whip out of his hand. 'The poor dears! Now you must promise not to be hard with them.'

'You don't know anything about dogs,' her brother said. 'So leave me alone. They're lazy and you've got to whip them to get anything out of them. That's their way. Ask one of those men.'

Mercedes looked at them, hoping they'd agree with her.

'They're very weak and exhausted, if you want to know,' replied one of the men. 'They need a rest.'

'Rest be damned[7],' said Hal.

But Mercedes sided[8] with her brother, rather than the stranger, and said, 'Never mind that man. You're driving our dogs, and you do what you think is best.'

Again Hal's whip fell upon the dogs. They tried again, getting down low to pull, using all of their strength. The sled stayed where it was. After two efforts[9] they stood still panting. The whip whistled amongst the dogs again, and Mercedes dropped on her knees in front of Buck, with tears in her eyes, and put her arms round his neck.

1 mountainous [ˋmaʊntənəs] (a.) 大如山的
2 demand [dɪˋmænd] (v.) 查問
3 annoyed [əˋnɔɪd] (a.) 氣惱的
4 top-heavy [ˋtɑp͵hɛvɪ] (a.) 頭重腳輕的
5 mush [mʌʃ] (int.) 快走（對拉雪橇的狗的吆喝聲）
6 creature [ˋkritʃɚ] (n.) 動物；家畜
7 damned [dæmd] (a.) 討厭的
8 side [saɪd] (v.) 同意；支持
9 effort [ˋɛfɚt] (n.) 努力

'You poor, poor dears,' she cried sympathetically[1], 'why don't you pull hard? Then you wouldn't be whipped.' Buck didn't like her, but he was feeling too miserable to resist[2] her, taking it as part of the day's miserable work.

One of the watchers finally spoke: 'It's not that I care what happens to you, but for the dogs' sakes[3] I just want to tell you that you can help by pushing the sled. The runners[4] are frozen to the ground.'

A third attempt was made, but this time, following the advice, the overloaded sled broke out of the ice and moved forward, while Hal whipped the dogs. A hundred meters ahead the path turned and sloped steeply into the main street so it would have been difficult for an experienced man to keep the top-heavy sled upright. As they turned, the sled went over, spilling[5] half of its load. The dogs didn't stop, and the lightened sled moved on its side behind them.

They were angry because of the bad treatment[6] they had received and the unjust load. Buck started to run and the team followed him. Hal cried 'Whoa[7]! Whoa!' but they didn't listen. He tripped[8] and was pulled off his feet. The sled ran over him, and the dogs dashed[9] on, adding to the happiness of Skaguay as they scattered[10] the rest of the equipment[11] along its main street.

1 sympathetically [ˌsɪmpəˋθɛtɪklɪ] (adv.) 同情地
2 resist [rɪˋzɪst] (v.) 抵抗
3 sake [sek] (n.) 理由
4 runner [ˋrʌnɚ] (n.) 滑道
5 spill [spɪl] (v.) 使散落
6 treatment [ˋtritmənt] (n.) 對待
7 whoa [hwo] (int.) 咳（叫馬停住或慢走）
8 trip [trɪp] (v.) 跌倒
9 dash [dæʃ] (v.) 急奔
10 scatter [ˋskætɚ] (v.) 散布
11 equipment [ɪˋkwɪpmənt] (n.) 裝備

41

Kind-hearted citizens[1] caught the dogs and collected the belongings[2]. They also gave advice: halve the load if they wanted to reach Dawson. Hal and his relations listened unwillingly[3], made camp and looked through their equipment. Those who helped them laughed that they had wanted to take canned[4] food, loads of blankets, the tent and so many dishes. Mercedes cried as her clothes were thrown out. In the end she threw out things that were really necessary.

When they had finished it was still a large load. Charles and Hal went out and bought six more dogs, which brought the team up to fourteen. But the new dogs were not very good, and seemed to know nothing. Buck and his comrades[5] looked on them with disgust[6], and though he quickly taught them their places and what not to do, he could not teach them what to do. They did not like the harness and the trail. Most of them found this strange new environment difficult, and they were not used to the bad treatment they had received.

With these hopeless new dogs, and the old team still worn out, the outlook[7] wasn't bright. The two men, however, were cheerful[8] and proud: they were doing things in style with fourteen dogs. They had seen many sleds come from and go to Dawson, but no sled had fourteen dogs.

In Arctic travel there was a reason why fourteen dogs should not pull one sled: one sled could not carry the food for fourteen dogs.

But Charles and Hal did not know this. They had worked the trip out with a pencil, so much food per[9] dog, so many dogs, so many days. For them it was all very simple.

1 citizen [ˋsɪtəzn̩] (n.) 居民
2 belongings [bəˋlɔŋɪŋz] (n.)〔複〕所攜帶之物
3 unwillingly [ʌnˋwɪlɪŋlɪ] (adv.) 不情願地
4 canned [kænd] (a.) 裝成罐頭的
5 comrade [ˋkɑmræd] (n.) 夥伴
6 disgust [dɪsˋgʌst] (n.) 憎惡
7 outlook [ˋaʊt͵lʊk] (n.) 展望
8 cheerful [ˋtʃɪrfəl] (a.) 興高采烈的
9 per [pɚ] (prep.) 每

THE TRIP

- What problems do you think lie ahead for Buck, the other dogs, and the people on this trip? Discuss with a partner.

Late next morning Buck led the team up the street. They were starting out dead tired. Four times he had covered the distance between Salt Water and Dawson. The knowledge that, exhausted, he was facing the same trail again, made him bitter. His heart was not in the work, nor was the heart of any dog. The new dogs were frightened, and none of the dogs had any confidence[1] in their masters.

Buck felt that these two men and the woman did not know how to do anything. As the days passed it was clear that they could not learn. They lacked order and discipline. It took them half the night to make their poor camp, and half the morning to pack up. They always loaded the sled so badly that they had to keep stopping to adjust[2] it. Some days they did not even travel fifteen kilometers. And on no day did they succeed in making half the distance used by the men as the basis of their dog-food calculations. So it was inevitable[3] that they would go short[4].

1 confidence [ˋkɑnfədəns] (n.) 信心
2 adjust [əˋdʒʌst] (v.) 調整
3 inevitable [ɪnˋɛvətəbl̩] (a.) 不可避免的
4 go short 發生短缺
5 overfeed [ˏovɚˋfid] (v.) 餵食過量（動詞三態：overfeed; overfed; overfed）
6 underfeed [ˏʌndɚˋfid] (v.) 餵食不足
7 appetite [ˋæpəˏtaɪt] (n.) 食欲
8 sack [sæk] (n.) 袋
9 obtain [əbˋten] (v.) 得到
10 cut down 削減
11 intend [ɪnˋtɛnd] (v.) 想要；打算
12 ration [ˋræʃən] (n.) 配給量；定量

They tried to speed up the journey by overfeeding[5] the dogs. Bringing the day nearer when underfeeding[6] would start. The new dogs had big appetites[7], and when Hal decided that the worn-out team was weak, he doubled their food. And then on top of this, Mercedes stole from the fish-sacks[8] and fed them behind Hal's back, because she felt sorry for the dogs. However it was not food that Buck and the huskies needed, but rest. And though they were going slowly, the heavy load they pulled took away their strength.

Then came the underfeeding. Hal realized one day that half of the dog-food was gone and only a quarter of the distance had been covered. And no more dog-food could be obtained[9]. So he cut down[10] on the intended[11] amount of food and tried to increase the distance they traveled every day. It was easy to give the dogs less food. But it was impossible to increase the distance they traveled when their owners were not able to get organized in the morning.

The first dog to go was Dub. His shoulder had never been treated and went from bad to worse, until finally Hal shot him with his Colt pistol. The new dogs were unable to survive on half rations[12] and soon six of them were dead.

44 And the people had problems, too. They became irritable[1] because they were in pain: their muscles ached[2]; their bones ached; their hearts ached. And so they were always angry. Charles and Hal fought all the time, each one believing he did more work than the other. Sometimes Mercedes sided with her husband and sometimes with her brother. The result was an unending[3] family quarrel[4]. And while they argued the fire remained unmade, the camp half prepared and the dogs unfed.

Mercedes found things especially hard. She was pretty and soft and she had been treated kindly all her life. She stopped worrying about the dogs, and because she was in pain and tired, she kept riding on the sled. She was pretty and soft, but she weighed eighty kilos. This was a serious extra weight for the weak and starving[5] dogs to pull. She rode for days, until the dogs fell down and the sled stood still. Charles and Hal begged her to get off and walk, and she wept[6] and said they were cruel.

MERCEDES

- You are Mercedes. How do you feel and why?
- What advice would you give her?

Because of their own misery, they ignored[7] the suffering of the dogs. At the Five Fingers the dog-food ran out, and a native American traded[8] a few kilos of frozen horse meat for the Colt pistol on Hal's belt. It was poor food, more like eating iron than meat.

And through it all Buck staggered[9] along at the head of the team as in a nightmare. He pulled when he could. When he could no longer pull, he fell down and remained down until the whip or the club got him up again. His fur was in a bad state; his bones were visible[10]. It was heartbreaking. But Buck's heart was unbreakable.

1 irritable [ˋɪrətəbḷ] (a.) 易怒的
2 ache [ek] (v.) 持續性的疼痛
3 unending [ʌnˋɛndɪŋ] (a.) 無止境的
4 quarrel [ˋkwɔrəl] (n.) 爭吵；不和
5 starving [ˋstɑrvɪŋ] (a.) 極饑餓的
6 weep [wip] (v.) 哭泣（動詞三態：weep; wept; wept）
7 ignore [ɪgˋnor] (v.) 忽視；不理會
8 trade [tred] (v.) 交換
9 stagger [ˋstægɚ] (v.) 蹣跚而行
10 visible [ˋvɪzəbḷ] (a.) 可見的

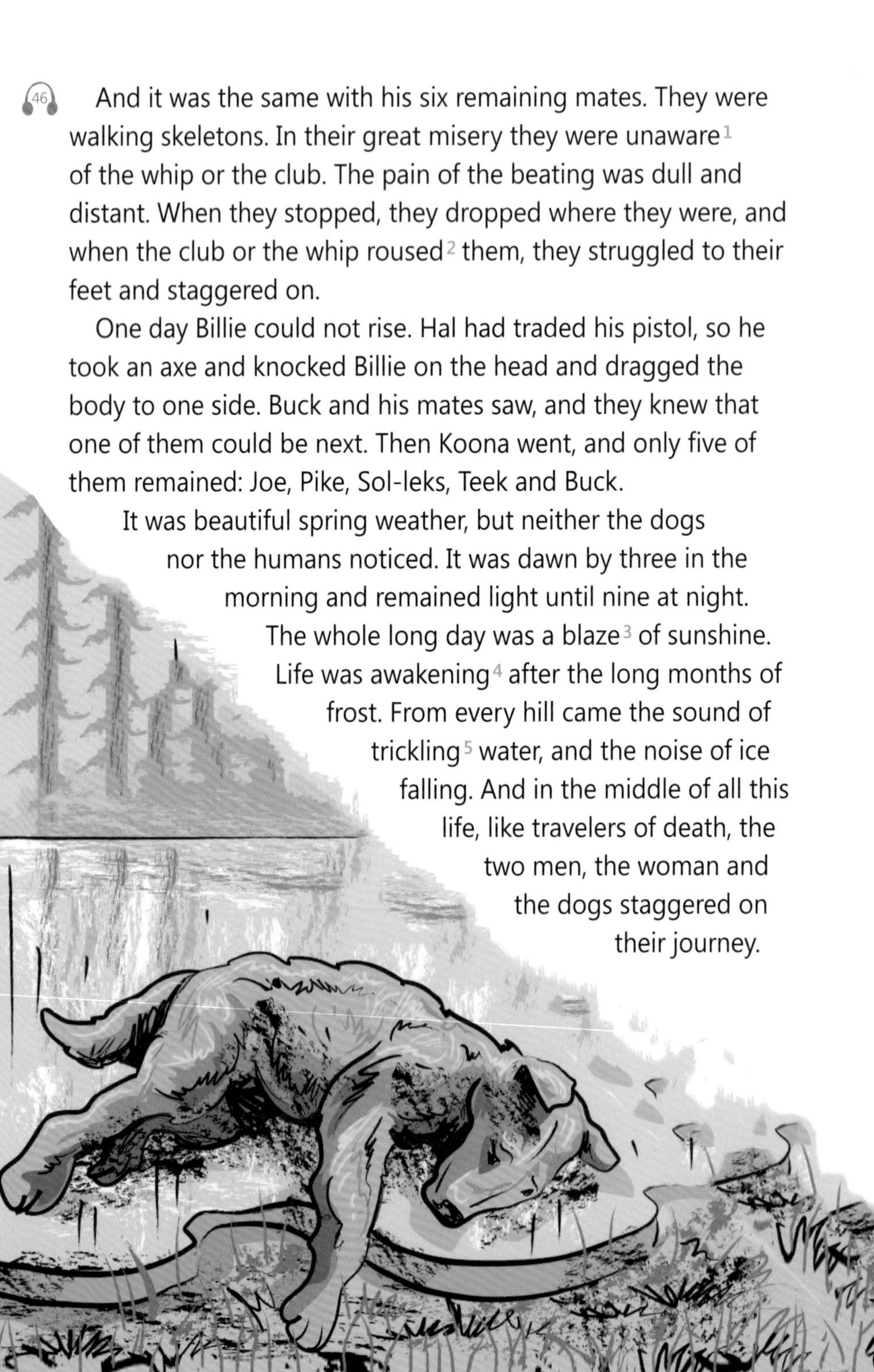

46 And it was the same with his six remaining mates. They were walking skeletons. In their great misery they were unaware[1] of the whip or the club. The pain of the beating was dull and distant. When they stopped, they dropped where they were, and when the club or the whip roused[2] them, they struggled to their feet and staggered on.

One day Billie could not rise. Hal had traded his pistol, so he took an axe and knocked Billie on the head and dragged the body to one side. Buck and his mates saw, and they knew that one of them could be next. Then Koona went, and only five of them remained: Joe, Pike, Sol-leks, Teek and Buck.

It was beautiful spring weather, but neither the dogs nor the humans noticed. It was dawn by three in the morning and remained light until nine at night. The whole long day was a blaze[3] of sunshine. Life was awakening[4] after the long months of frost. From every hill came the sound of trickling[5] water, and the noise of ice falling. And in the middle of all this life, like travelers of death, the two men, the woman and the dogs staggered on their journey.

With the dogs falling, Mercedes weeping and riding, Hal swearing[6] and Charles' eyes watering, they staggered into John Thornton's camp at the mouth of the White River. When they stopped the dogs dropped down as though they were dead. Thornton listened and gave monosyllabic[7] answers to questions, and brief advice, knowing that it was unlikely to be followed.

'In Skaguay they said that the ice was starting to break up and that we should stop and wait,' said Hal. 'But they also told us that we couldn't get to White River and here we are.'

'They told you the truth,' said Thornton. 'I tell you honestly that I wouldn't risk my life on that ice for all the gold in Alaska.'

'No!' said Hal. 'We'll go to Dawson. Get up, Buck! Mush!'

He cracked[8] his whip on the dogs, and one by one. They all stood up except Buck. Buck lay quietly where he had fallen. Hal whipped him again and again, but he didn't whine[9] or struggle. Several times Thornton started to speak, but changed his mind.

THORNTON

- What do you think Thornton was going to say?
- What would you say to Hal?

1 unaware [ˌʌnəˋwɛr] (a.) 無感的
2 rouse [raʊz] (v.) 弄醒
3 blaze [blez] (n.) 強光
4 awakening [əˋwekənɪŋ] (a.) 正在醒過來的；萌動中的
5 trickle [ˋtrɪkḷ] (v.) 細細地流
6 swear [swɛr] (v.) 發誓
7 monosyllabic [ˌmɑnəsəˋlæbɪk] (a.) 單音節的
8 crack [kræk] (v.) 猛擊
9 whine [hwaɪn] (v.) 發哀鳴聲

1 drive sb into a rage 惹怒某人
2 doom [dum] (n.) 厄運
3 disaster [dɪˋzæstɚ] (n.) 災難
4 at hand 即將到來的
5 spark [spɑrk] (n.) 火花
6 intention [ɪnˋtɛnʃən] (n.) 意圖
7 handle [ˋhændḷ] (n.) 柄

This was the first time Buck had failed, and it drove Hal into a rage[1]. He got his club and beat Buck. But Buck had a feeling of doom[2]. He had felt the weak ice under his feet and sensed disaster[3] close at hand[4], out there on the ice where his master wanted to go. So Buck refused to move. He had suffered so greatly and was so weak, that being hit with the club hardly hurt him. As the beating went on, the spark[5] of life inside him went down, and nearly went out. It no longer seemed to be his body where the club was falling; it seemed so far away.

And then suddenly, without warning, shouting more like an animal than a human, John Thornton jumped on Hal, who was thrown backwards. Mercedes screamed. Thornton stood over Buck. He was struggling to control himself, too angry to speak.

'If you hit that dog again, I'll kill you,' he at last managed to say in a choking voice.

'It's my dog,' Hal replied, wiping the blood from his mouth. 'Get out of my way, or I'll kill you. I'm going to Dawson.'

Thornton stood between him and Buck, and showed no intention[6] of getting out of the way. Hal took out his hunting-knife. Mercedes screamed and cried. Thornton hit Hal's hand with an axe handle[7] he was holding, knocking the knife to the ground. He hit his hand again as Hal tried to pick it up. Then Thornton picked up the knife himself and cut Buck's harness with it.

Hal could fight no more. Besides, his sister had run into his arms, and Buck was too near dead to be of further use in pulling the sled. A few minutes later they pulled off and down the river.

49

Buck heard them go and raised his head to see. Pike was leading, Sol-leks was at the back, and between were Joe and Teek. They were limping[1] and staggering. Mercedes was riding on the loaded sled, with Hal guiding it and Charles stumbling[2] along behind.

As Buck watched them, Thornton knelt[3] beside him and with rough[4], kind hands searched for broken bones. He found nothing broken but Buck was in a state of terrible starvation[5]. By now the sled was half a kilometer away. Dog and man watched as it crawled over the ice. Suddenly, they saw its back end drop down. They heard Mercedes scream and saw Charles try to turn and run back, and then a complete section of the ice broke and dogs and humans disappeared. A huge hole was all there was. John Thornton and Buck looked at each other.

'You poor creature,' said John Thornton, and Buck licked his hand.

BUCK

- You are Buck. How do you feel now? Tell a partner.

1 limp [lɪmp] (v.) 一瘸一拐地走
2 stumble [ˋstʌmbḷ] (v.) 蹣跚而行
3 kneel [nil] (v.) 跪著（動詞三態：kneel; knelt / kneeled; knelt / kneeled）
4 rough [rʌf] (a.) 粗糙的
5 starvation [stɑrˋveʃən] (n.) 飢餓

FOR THE LOVE OF A MAN

50 Buck started to relax, lying by the river bank through the long spring days, watching the running water, listening to the songs of the birds and the hum[1] of nature. And he slowly got his strength back. A rest is a good thing after travelling four thousand five hundred kilometers. Buck got lazy as his wounds healed[2], his muscles grew again, and the flesh came back over his bones. He also made friends with Skeet, an Irish setter[3], and Nig, a huge black dog, who were already living with John Thornton. And Buck came to love John Thornton.

This man had saved his life, and he was also the ideal[4] master. He looked after the dogs as if they were his children. He never forgot to say something when he saw them, and to sit down and talk to them. Buck lay for hours at Thornton's feet, looking up into his face and following his expressions[5] as they changed.

Buck was afraid of losing John Thornton, in the way he had lost all his other masters. But even though he loved Thornton, and behaved in ways that made him seem civilized[6], the primitiveness[7] which he had learned in the Northland remained alive inside him. He was a wild thing, come in from the wild to sit by John Thornton's fire.

1 hum [hʌm] (n.) 嗡嗡聲
2 heal [hil] (v.) 痊癒
3 setter [ˋsɛtɚ] (n.) 一種長毛獵犬
4 ideal [aɪˋdiəl] (a.) 理想的；完美的
5 expression [ɪkˋsprɛʃən] (n.) 表情
6 civilized [ˋsɪvə͵laɪzd] (a.) 文明的；開化的
7 primitiveness [ˋprɪmətɪvnɪs] (n.) 原始
8 supremacy [səˋprɛməsɪ] (n.) 最高地位
9 exceptional [ɪkˋsɛpʃənl̩] (a.) 卓越的
10 merciless [ˋmɝsɪlɪs] (a.) 無情的

His face and body were covered by the marks of the fights he had had. Buck still fought as fiercely as ever, but now he fought more cleverly. He didn't fight with Skeet and Nig, who were too good-natured, and besides, they also belonged to John Thornton. But any strange dog quickly accepted Buck's supremacy[8] or he was struggling for his life against this exceptional[9] fighter. And Buck was merciless[10]. He never gave up an advantage or stood back from a dying enemy. He had learned well, and he knew there was no middle way. He must master or be mastered. Kill or be killed, eat or be eaten, was the law. And it was a law that Buck obeyed.

CHANGES IN BUCK

- How has Buck changed from the start of the story?
- What kind of dog is he now?

52

He sat by John Thornton's fire, a broad-chested dog with white teeth and long fur, but behind him were the shadows of all sorts of dogs, half-wolves and wild wolves. And they called to him, so that each day his relationship with people moved further away. Deep in the forest a call was sounding. When he heard it, he felt that he should leave the fire and run into the forest, not knowing where he was going or why. But then his love for John Thornton pulled him back again. But it was only for Thornton he stayed. Other people were nothing to him.

Pete and Hans, Thornton's business partners, understood the relationship between Buck and Thornton very well.

'I wouldn't like to be the man that attacks Thornton while Buck's around,' said Pete one day.

And before the end of the year, in Circle City, Pete's thoughts were shown to be true. 'Black' Burton, a bad-tempered[1] and dangerous man, had been picking a fight with an inexperienced[2] young man. Thornton stepped between them to stop it while Buck was watching from the corner of the room. Burton punched[3] Thornton unexpectedly and hard, and Thornton was sent flying across the room.

Those who were watching heard a roar, and they saw Buck jumping for Burton's throat. The man saved his life by putting out his arm, but he was thrown onto the floor with Buck on top of him. Buck let go[4] of the arm and went for[5] the throat again and this time tore[6] it open. Then the crowd[7] pulled Buck off. Buck walked up and down nearby, growling and looking for another chance to attack, while the doctor examined Burton.

1 bad-tempered [ˋbædˋtɛmpɚd] (a.) 脾氣不好的
2 inexperienced [ˌɪnɪkˋspɪrɪənst] (a.) 經驗不足的
3 punch [pʌntʃ] (v.) 用拳猛擊
4 let go 放開
5 go for 攻擊
6 tear [tɛr] (v.) 撕扯（動詞三態：tear; tore; torn）
7 crowd [kraʊd] (n.) 人群

53 It was agreed that Buck had had a good reason to attack, so he wasn't punished. But his reputation[1] grew and his name spread[2] through every camp in Alaska.

Later that autumn, Thornton and his two partners were taking a narrow boat down a difficult river. Thornton was in the boat, and Pete and Hans were on the bank with a rope to stop the boat being carried away.

Buck was on the bank, anxiously watching his master. Unexpectedly, the water carried the boat faster, the rope was pulled tight, and Thornton was thrown into the river. Buck dived[3] into the water and soon caught up with his master. Thornton held onto Buck's tail while the dog started swimming strongly for the side.

But the river was going so fast, they were being carried close to the most dangerous, rocky place. Thornton managed to catch hold of a rock in the river, and Buck, with difficulty, swam[4] to the bank, and was pulled out by Hans and Pete.

They then attached[5] the rope to Buck's shoulders, and he tried to swim out to where Thornton was hanging on to the rock. However he got carried away by the current[6], and nearly drowned[7] before Pete and Hans pulled him out. Thornton couldn't hang on much longer, so Buck tried again and went fast down to Thornton, who grabbed[8] his neck. Then the two of them were pulled in on the rope by Hans and Pete. They had been battered[9] by the water and the rocks, and Buck had three ribs[10] broken, but he had saved his master's life.

DANGER

- Have you ever been in a dangerous situation? Who helped you?
- Have you ever helped anyone out of danger? Describe your feelings to a partner.

1 reputation [ˏrɛpjəˋteʃən] (n.) 名聲
2 spread [sprɛd] (v.) 展開；散布（動詞三態：spread; spread; spread）
3 dive [daɪv] (v.) 跳水；俯衝
4 swim [swɪm] (v.) 游泳（動詞三態：swim; swam; swum）
5 attach [əˋtætʃ] (v.) 繫上
6 current [ˋkɝənt] (n.) 水流
7 drown [draʊn] (v.) 淹死；淹沒
8 grab [græb] (v.) 攫取
9 batter [ˋbætɚ] (v.) 連續猛擊
10 rib [rɪb] (n.) 肋骨

54

Later on that year in Dawson, Buck did another important thing. Thornton was in a bar[1] one night when a man said that his dog could start a sled alone, with three hundred kilos on it. Another man, called Matthewson, said his could do so with four hundred kilos on it.

'That's nothing,' said John Thornton. 'Buck can start a sled with five hundred kilos on it.'

'What, and break it out of the ice and snow?' asked Matthewson. 'And pull it for one hundred meters?'

'And do that, too,' answered Thornton coolly[2].

'Well,' said Matthewson. 'I bet you one thousand dollars that he can't. There it is.' And he banged[3] a bag of gold dust down on the bar.

Thornton did not actually know whether Buck could do what he'd said, but he had often thought he would be able to. Even so it was a terribly large amount to pull. And also, neither he nor Pete nor Hans had one thousand dollars to bet with.

'I've got a sled standing outside now, with ten fifty kilo sacks on it,' Matthewson said, 'so we can easily try.'

Thornton looked at the faces of all the men in the bar watching him. Then he saw an old friend of his who had got rich by finding gold.

'Can you lend me a thousand?' he asked, in a whisper[4].

'Sure,' answered his friend, putting the money on the bar. 'But I'm not sure the dog can really do it.'

1 bar [bɑr] (n.) 酒吧
2 coolly [ˋkulɪ] (adv.) 冷靜地
3 bang [bæŋ] (v.) 發出砰的一聲
4 whisper [ˋhwɪspɚ] (n.) 私語
5 intense [ɪnˋtɛns] (a.) 劇烈的
6 bet on sth 打賭某事
7 odds [ɑds] (n.)〔複〕投注賠率
8 three to one 三比一
9 sledge [slɛdʒ] (n.) 雪橇

55 Matthewson's sled was loaded with ten fifty kilo sacks of flour. It was frozen into the snow after standing in the intense[5] cold for more than two hours. Lots of men gathered to watch, and started betting on[6] whether Buck could move it or not. The odds[7] were three to one[8] against him doing it. Matthewson offered him another thousand dollar bet, at the three-to-one odds. Thornton and his partners only had two hundred between them, but they bet that against Matthewson's six hundred dollars.

So Buck was harnessed on his own to the sledge[9]. He felt the excitement, and knew that in some way he must do a great thing for John Thornton. Buck was in perfect condition. All those watching recognized this, but they still didn't think he could do it. Thornton went to Buck, and took his head between his two hands, and whispered in his ear: 'As you love me, Buck.'

56

Thornton stood up and stepped back. 'Now, Buck,' he said.

'Gee!' shouted Thornton, and Buck moved hard to the right, shaking the load, and a cracking noise was heard.

'Haw[1]!' Thornton commanded[2]. And Buck repeated the action to the left side, with similar noises from the ice. The sled was broken out of the ice.

'Now, MUSH!' shouted Thornton, and Buck started, head low, chest near the ground, feet slipping[3] on the snow at first, but centimeter by centimeter the huge weight slid forward until Buck had it moving steadily along. The crowd

1 haw [hɔ] (int.)（對馬、牛發令）左轉
2 command [kəˋmænd] (v.) 命令；指揮
3 slip [slɪp] (v.) 滑動

had held their breath, but now they started shouting, until a huge roar went up when he crossed the one hundred meter line.

Thornton ran up to Buck and fell on his knees beside him, and they put head against head and moved backwards and forwards together. When Thornton finally stood up tears were rolling down his face.

THE SOUNDING OF THE CALL

57 Buck earned one thousand six hundred dollars in five minutes for John Thornton. And he made it possible for his master to travel with his partners to look for an old lost gold mine. Many men had searched for it and many had never returned from their trip. Thornton, Pete and Hans set off with a team of Buck and six other dogs, and sledded[1] one hundred kilometers up the Yukon, into the Stewart River, and continued until it became a small stream high up in the mountains.

John Thornton was unafraid of the wild. He could walk deep into the wilderness[2], going wherever he pleased for as long as he pleased. He was never in a hurry, hunting his food during the journey. If he failed to find anything to eat, he kept travelling, knowing that sooner or later he would find it. So on this trip, the sled was mostly loaded with ammunition[3] for the guns and tools.

To Buck the hunting and fishing and indefinite[4] wandering[5] through strange places was an endless delight. For several weeks they would travel steadily[6]. For endless weeks they would camp, while the men looked for gold. Sometimes they were hungry, sometimes they had huge feasts[7]. Summer arrived, and the dogs and men put packs on their backs and floated[8] across blue mountain lakes, and went up or down unknown rivers on boats they had made from the forests around them.

1 sled [slɛd] (v.) 用雪橇運
2 wilderness [ˋwɪldɚnɪs] (n.) 荒野；荒漠
3 ammunition [ˏæmjəˋnɪʃən] (n.) 彈藥
4 indefinite [ɪnˋdɛfənɪt] (a.) 不確定的
5 wander [ˋwɑndɚ] (v.) 漫遊
6 steadily [ˋstɛdəlɪ] (adv.) 穩定地
7 feast [fist] (n.) 盛宴
8 float [flot] (v.) 漂浮

58 Time passed as they moved backwards and forwards across this unmapped[1] wild country, where there were no men, but where men had been, if the story of the lost mine was true. They wandered for a summer and another winter.

When spring came once more, they didn't find the lost mine, but a valley where there was gold shining through the stones at the sides of the river. They stopped wandering, and each day that they worked they earned themselves thousands of dollars in clean gold dust and nuggets[2]. And they worked every day. The gold was put into leather sacks, twenty-five kilos per sack, and piled[3] outside the shelter they had built.

There was nothing for the dogs to do, and Buck spent long hours thinking by the fire. The vision[4] of the short-legged hairy man came to him more frequently. Now that there was little work to be done, Buck often lay[5] by the fire, and wandered with him in that other world which he remembered.

The hairy man was afraid, always watching, ready to run when danger appeared. He walked silently with Buck through the forests. Sometimes the man would jump into the trees and swing[6] from branch[7] to branch, never falling, seeming as much at home in the trees as on the ground.

And along with these visions, Buck felt the call that came from deep inside the forests. It filled him with strange desires for things that he didn't know. Sometimes he would jump up and disappear for hours. He walked along dry rivers, watching the birds, reading the sounds and signs as a man may read a book. And he looked for the mysterious[8] thing that called him all the time, waking or sleeping. It was calling for him to come.

1 unmapped [ʌnˋmæpt] (a.) 地圖上未標示的
2 nugget [ˋnʌgɪt] (n.) 天然金塊；礦塊
3 pile [paɪl] (v.) 堆積
4 vision [ˋvɪʒən] (n.) 所見事物
5 lie [laɪ] (v.) 躺（動詞三態：lie; lay; lain）
6 swing [swɪŋ] (v.) 擺盪（動詞三態：swing; swung; swung）
7 branch [bræntʃ] (n.) 樹枝
8 mysterious [mɪsˋtɪrɪəs] (a.) 神祕的

THE CALL

- What is the 'mysterious thing that called'?
- Is it a real 'call', like a voice, or something else?
- Think of the title of the book. Discuss with a partner.

One night he jumped from his sleep suddenly, scenting[1] the air. He heard the call coming from the forest – it was a long howl, like, yet unlike, any noise made by a husky dog. He ran through the sleeping camp and into the woods. As he got closer to the cry he went more slowly, taking care in every movement, till he came to an open place among the trees. Then he saw, sitting with its nose pointed to the sky, a long, thin timber wolf[2].

Buck had made no noise, but the wolf stopped its howling and tried to sense[3] him. Buck walked out into the open[4], each movement showing both threat and friendliness. But the wolf ran away. Buck followed and overtook[5] him. He cornered[6] the wolf, who turned, snapping[7] his teeth.

Buck did not attack, but circled around and made friendly advances[8]. The wolf was suspicious[9] and afraid, for Buck was three times bigger than him. When he saw his chance, he rushed away and the chase resumed[10]. Many times he was cornered, and in the end Buck was rewarded[11], because the wolf, finding that Buck meant him no harm, finally sniffed noses with him. Then they played about and finally the wolf walked off in a way which showed that he was going somewhere and that he wanted Buck to follow him.

From the top of the valley they came down into level[12] country where there were great stretches[13] of forest and many streams. They ran side by side, hour after hour, as the sun was rising and the day was getting warmer. Buck was extremely[14] happy. He knew he was at last answering the call, running by the side of his wild brother towards the place where the call surely came from. Old memories came into his head. He had done this before in that other world. He was doing it again now, running free with the earth under his feet and the wide sky overhead[15].

They stopped by a stream to drink, and Buck remembered John Thornton. He sat down. The wolf started towards the place from which the call surely came, then returned to him, sniffing noses and trying to encourage[16] him. But Buck turned round and started slowly back. For the better part of an hour the wild brother ran by his side, whining softly. Then he sat down, pointed his nose upward, and howled. It was a sad and lonely sound. As Buck kept walking, he heard it growing fainter until it was lost in the distance.

BUCK'S DECISION

- Why does Buck decide to leave the wolf?
- Have you ever made a difficult decision? What was it? Why was it difficult? Tell a partner.

1 scent [sɛnt] (v.) 嗅
2 timber wolf 北美大灰狼
3 sense [sɛns] (v.) 感覺
4 open [`opən] (n.) 曠野；空地
5 overtake [͵ovɚ`tek] (v.) 趕上（動詞三態：overtake; overtook; overtaken）
6 corner [`kɔrnɚ] (v.) 把……逼到角落
7 snap [snæp] (v.) 使發劈啪聲
8 advance [əd`væns] (n.) 前進
9 suspicious [sə`spɪʃəs] (a.) 猜疑的
10 resume [rɪ`zjum] (v.) 重新開始；繼續
11 reward [rɪ`wɔrd] (v.) 報答；獎賞
12 level [`lɛvḷ] (a.) 平坦的
13 stretch [strɛtʃ] (n.) 連綿
14 extremely [ɪk`strimlɪ] (adv.) 極度的
15 overhead [`ovɚ`hɛd] (adv.) 在頭頂上
16 encourage [ɪn`kɝɪdʒ] (v.) 鼓勵

John Thornton was eating dinner when Buck ran back into the camp and jumped on him, full of affection, pushing him over and licking his face. For two days and nights, Buck never left camp or let Thornton out of his sight. He followed him at work, watched while he ate, saw him into bed at night and out of it again next morning. But after two days the call of the forest began to sound more strongly than ever. Buck felt restless[1], and he thought about his wild brother, and the land beyond the valley, and running side-by-side with the other wolves. Once again he started wandering in the woods, but his wild brother didn't come back and the sad howl was never heard again.

He began to sleep out at night, staying away for days at a time, looking without success for his wild brother. He killed his meat as he traveled, moving with an easy step that never seemed to tire[3]. He fished for salmon[2] in a stream, and also killed a large black bear in a hard fight.

The desire for blood became stronger than ever before. He was a killer, a thing that hunted other animals, living on things that lived. He got his meat unaided[3], alone, because of his own strength and ability. And he survived well in a difficult environment where only the strong survived. Apart from the brown mark on his nose and the white hair that ran down his chest, he looked almost like a gigantic[4] wolf. He was at his peak[5], physically[6] and mentally[7]. He saw, decided and responded[8], all in the same moment.

1 restless [ˋrɛstlɪs] (a.) 焦躁不安的
2 salmon [ˋsæmən] (n.) 鮭魚
3 unaided [ʌnˋedɪd] (a.) 獨立的
4 gigantic [dʒaɪˋgæntɪk] (a.) 巨大的
5 peak [pik] (n.) 巔峰
6 physically [ˋfɪzɪkḷɪ] (adv.) 身體上
7 mentally [ˋmɛntḷɪ] (adv.) 精神上
8 respond [rɪˋspɑnd] (v.) 回應

62 'There was never a dog like him,' said John Thornton one day, as the three partners watched Buck walking out of the camp.

They saw him walk out of the camp, but they did not see the terrible change that happened as soon as he was inside the forest. At once[1] he became a wild thing, moving softly like a cat, almost like a shadow that appeared and disappeared among other shadows. He knew how to use the cover of bushes[2] and trees. He could take game[3] birds from the nest, kill rabbits as they slept, and catch squirrels[4] as they ran for the trees; fish in open pools were too slow for him.

As autumn came, the moose[5] appeared in larger numbers, moving from the colder tops to the valleys. Buck had already killed a partly grown[6] moose that he'd found on its own, but he greatly wanted to kill a larger and more difficult animal. One day, at the top of the valley he found a herd[7] of twenty moose amongst which was a great male. He stood two meters from the ground, and was as terrible an enemy as even Buck could desire. The moose shook his huge horns[8], which were over two meters across, and roared with anger when he saw Buck.

The first thing that Buck did was to separate the male from the rest of the herd. This was not easy. Every time Buck annoyed[9] the male enough for it to run at him, several young males would run at Buck and help the big male back into the herd. But Buck was patient[10], like all hunting animals, and for half a day he followed the herd, attacking them from all sides, and separating the large male from the herd. As the day passed, the young males would go to help him less and less.

As night started to fall, the male was left on his own facing Buck, as the herd moved off into the darkness, and he could not follow because Buck prevented him. He weighed around 1,150 kilos, and had lived a long, strong life full of fights and struggle, and here he faced death from the teeth of an animal whose head was only as high as his knees.

From then on Buck never left the huge male moose, never gave him a moment's rest, never let him eat or drink. When the moose tried to run away, Buck just followed behind him, running easily, then lying down when the moose stood still[11], and attacking fiercely whenever he tried to eat or drink.

The moose's great head dropped and its movements grew weaker. He started standing for long periods, with his nose to the ground, so Buck had time to get water for himself. And while he rested and waited, Buck sensed that a change was coming over the land, that other kinds of life were coming. He heard nothing and saw nothing, yet he knew that the land was somehow different. He decided to investigate[12] after he had finished with the moose.

1 at once 立刻
2 bush [bʊʃ] (n.) 灌木叢
3 game [gem] (n.) 獵物
4 squirrel [ˋskwɝəl] (n.) 松鼠
5 moose [mus] (n.) 麋鹿
6 grown [gron] (a.) 長大了的
7 herd [hɝd] (n.) 畜群
8 horn [hɔrn] (n.) 角
9 annoy [əˋnɔɪ] (v.) 惹惱；打攪
10 patient [ˋpeʃənt] (a.) 耐心的
11 still [stɪl] (adv.) 靜止地
12 investigate [ɪnˋvɛstə͵get] (v.) 調查

64

At last, at the end of the fourth day, he pulled the great moose down. For a day and a night he remained by the kill, eating and sleeping. Then, rested, refreshed[1] and strong, he turned back towards the camp and John Thornton. He started his easy walk and went on, hour after hour, never losing his way, heading[2] straight for home through strange country.

1 refreshed [rɪˋfrɛʃɪd] (a.) 消除疲勞的
2 head [hɛd] (v.) 向……出發
3 message [ˋmɛsɪdʒ] (n.) 訊息；消息

As he continued he became increasingly conscious of the change in the land. There was life around which was different to that which had been there in the summer. The birds and squirrels talked about it, even the wind whispered of it. Several times he stopped and took the message[3] in great sniffs of air, reading things which made him move with greater speed. He was filled with a sense of danger and disaster happening. And as he finally crossed the top of the hills, and went down into his valley, he moved more carefully.

BUCK'S SIXTH SENSE

- What do you think Buck senses? What has happened?
- What is going to happen?

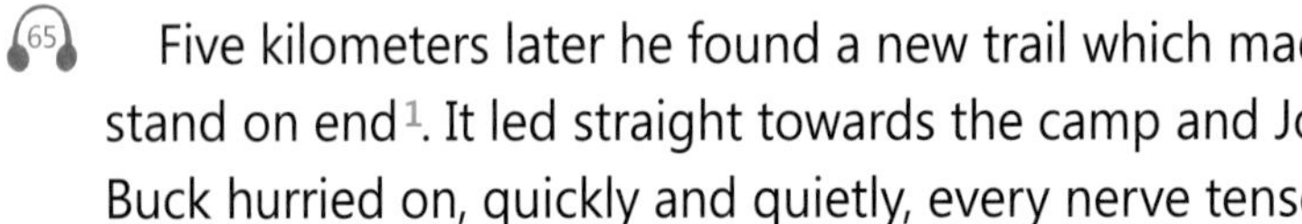

Five kilometers later he found a new trail which made his hair stand on end[1]. It led straight towards the camp and John Thornton. Buck hurried on, quickly and quietly, every nerve tense. He was alert to all the details[2] he sensed. They told him a complete[3] story – everything except the end. He noticed how silent the forest was. Then his nose pulled him to one side, and he found Nig lying on his side. The dog was dead, with an arrow through his body.

A little later he found one of the sled-dogs almost dead on the trail. Buck moved on without stopping. From the camp he could hear the faint sound of many voices, rising and falling in a chant.

1 make one's hair stand on end 使某人毛骨悚然
2 detail [ˋditel] (n.) 細節
3 complete [kəmˋplit] (a.) 完整的
4 clearing [ˋklɪrɪŋ] (n.) 林中的空地
5 arrow [ˋæro] (n.) 箭
6 lose one's head 驚慌失措
7 hurricane [ˋhɝɪˏken] (n.) 暴風雨
8 motion [ˋmoʃən] (n.) 移動；動作
9 panic [ˋpænɪk] (n.) 恐慌
10 terror [ˋtɛrɚ] (n.) 恐怖；驚駭

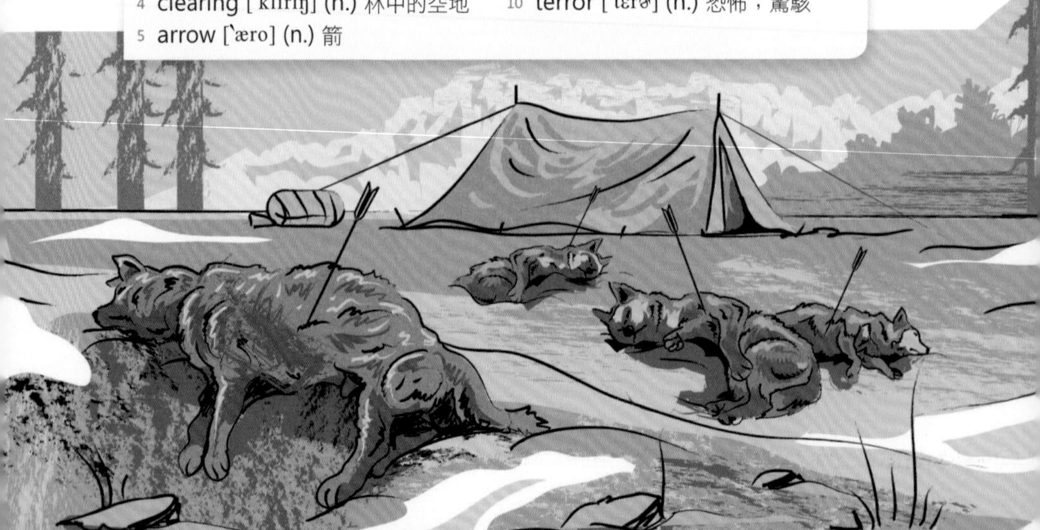

66 As he crawled on his stomach to the edge of the clearing[4] where the camp was, he found Hans lying dead with his body full of arrows[5]. Then as he looked up, what he saw made him so angry that he let his passion take over from his cunning and reason. It was because of his great love for John Thornton that he lost his head[6].

The Yeehat Indians were dancing around the camp hut when they heard Buck's roar of anger. They turned to see an animal they had never seen before rushing at them like a hurricane[7]. He threw himself at their leader and ripped out his throat, and then did the same with the next man. There was no stopping him. He ran at them, biting and tearing and destroying, in constant motion[8]. When the Yeehats tried to shoot him, they missed and their arrows hit other Indians. In panic[9] and terror[10] they ran for the woods, believing Buck to be an Evil Spirit.

67 Buck ran after them as they raced[1] through the trees, pulling them down like deer. It was a terrible day for the Yeehats. They ran off far and wide over the country, and it was only a week later that the last of the survivors[2] got together again and counted their losses[3]. As for Buck, he got tired of the chase, and returned to the desolate[4] camp. He found Pete, who was dead in his blankets. Thornton's desperate struggle was written all over the earth. Buck scented every detail of it down to the edge of a deep pool. Skeet, faithful[5] to the last, lay dead by the edge of the water. John Thornton lay in the pool's muddy[6] water. Buck followed his trace[7] into the water, but he could find no trace of his master that led away from it.

All day Buck lay by the pool, or walked restlessly around the camp. He knew about death, and he knew that John Thornton was dead. It left a great painful emptiness[8] inside him, like a hunger which no food could fill. At times, when he looked at the bodies of the dead Yeehats, he forgot the pain, and he felt proud of himself. He had killed man, the greatest game of all. He sniffed the bodies. They had died so easily. It was harder to kill a husky dog than them. They could not match[9] him without their arrows and clubs. From then onwards he would only be afraid of them if they had arrows and clubs in their hands.

Night came, and a full moon rose over the trees into the sky. As he lay by the pool, thinking and mourning[10], Buck became alive to new life in the forest. He stood up, listening and scenting. From far away drifted[11] a faint, sharp yelp, followed by others. As the moments passed the yelps grew closer and louder. Buck knew them as things heard in that other world that had stayed in his memory.

1 race [res] (v.) 全速行進
2 survivor [sɚˋvaɪvɚ] (n.) 倖存者
3 loss [lɔs] (n.) 傷亡或被擄的人數
4 desolate [ˋdɛsḷət] (a.) 荒蕪的
5 faithful [ˋfeθfəl] (a.) 忠實的；忠誠的
6 muddy [ˋmʌdɪ] (a.) 泥濘的
7 trace [tres] (n.) 痕跡
8 emptiness [ˋɛmptɪnɪs] (n.) 空虛
9 match [mætʃ] (v.) 敵得過
10 mourn [morn] (v.) 哀痛
11 drift [drɪft] (v.) 漂蕩

He walked into the center of the open space and listened. It was the call, the many-noted call, pulling him more than ever. And, as never before, he was ready to obey it. John Thornton was dead. The last tie[1] was broken. Man and his wishes no longer held Buck.

THE CALL OF THE WILD

- What has changed in Buck now? Why?
- What do you think he is going to do?

Hunting for meat and following the migrating[2] moose, the wolf pack[3] had crossed over from the land of streams and forests into Buck's valley. They poured into the clearing like a silver stream in the moonlight. Buck stood, motionless[4] as a statue[5] in the middle, waiting for them. They were quietened[6], so still and large he stood, and a moment's pause[7] fell. Then one wolf jumped at him, and like a flash[8], Buck struck, breaking his neck. Then Buck stood still again, as the wolf died in front of him. Three others tried, one after the other, and immediately crawled back, covered in blood from cut throats or shoulders.

This was enough to make the whole pack attack him. But Buck was fast and agile[9]. Snapping and tearing, he was everywhere at once. To stop them getting behind him, he moved backwards, down past the pool, and along a bank that men had made when they were mining[10]. Finally he got into a corner, protected on three sides and with nothing to do but face the front.

1 tie [taɪ] (n.) 關係；連繫
2 migrate [ˋmaɪˏgret] (v.) 遷移
3 pack [pæk] (n.) 群；隊
4 motionless [ˋmoʃənlɪs] (a.) 靜止不動的
5 statue [ˋstætʃu] (n.) 雕像
6 quieten [ˋkaɪətn̩] (v.) 使安靜
7 pause [pɔz] (n.) 暫停
8 flash [flæʃ] (n.) 閃光
9 agile [ˋædʒaɪl] (a.) 敏捷的
10 mine [maɪn] (v.) 挖坑道

69 And so well did he face it, that at the end of half an hour, the wolves drew back[1], defeated[2]. They lay or stood, watching Buck. One wolf, thin and grey, walked carefully towards him in a friendly way, and Buck recognized the wild brother with whom he had run night and day. He was whining softly, and as Buck whined, they touched noses.

Then an old scarred[3] wolf came forward and sniffed noses with Buck. The old wolf then sat down, pointed his nose at the moon and started the long wolf howl. The others all sat down and howled. And now the call came to Buck and it was unmistakable[4]. He, too, sat down and howled. This over, he came out of his corner, and the pack crowded round him in a half-friendly, half-savage way. The leaders yelped, and the pack moved away into the woods. And Buck ran with them, side by side with his wild brother, yelping as he ran.

And here the story of Buck could end. But it was not long before the Yeehat Indians noticed a change in the timber wolves. Some of them had patches[5] of brown on their heads and noses, and a white line down their chests. But more than that, the Yeehats tell of a Ghost Dog that runs at the head of the pack. They are afraid of this Ghost Dog, because it is more cunning than they are. It steals from their camps in hard winters, takes food from their traps, kills their dogs and stands up to[6] their bravest hunters.

But the story gets worse. There are hunters who never return to the camp. They are found with their throats cut open and footprints around them in the snow which are larger than any wolf prints. And each autumn, when the Yeehats follow the moose, there is a certain valley which they never enter. And they become sad when they talk over the fire of how the Evil Spirit selected that valley to live in.

1 draw back 退縮；撤回
2 defeat [dɪ`fit] (v.) 擊敗
3 scarred [skɑrd] (a.) 有疤痕的
4 unmistakable [͵ʌnmə`stekəbl̩] (a.) 清楚的
5 patch [pætʃ] (n.) 斑點
6 stand up to 勇敢地面對

THE GHOST DOG

- Who is the 'Ghost Dog'?
- What legends or stories are in your culture?
- What legends do you know? Share with a partner.

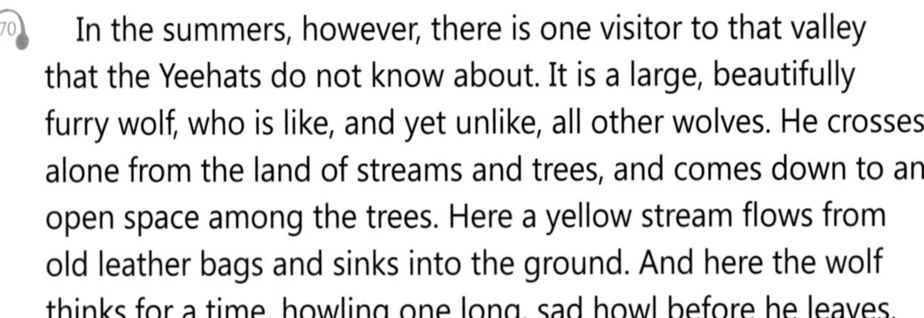

In the summers, however, there is one visitor to that valley that the Yeehats do not know about. It is a large, beautifully furry wolf, who is like, and yet unlike, all other wolves. He crosses alone from the land of streams and trees, and comes down to an open space among the trees. Here a yellow stream flows from old leather bags and sinks into the ground. And here the wolf thinks for a time, howling one long, sad howl before he leaves.

But he is not always alone. When the long winter nights come the wolves follow their meat into the lower valleys. Then he may be seen running at the head of the pack through the pale moonlight. He is gigantic and his great throat howls out the song of the younger world, which is the song of the pack.

After Reading

A Personal Response

1. What did you think of the story? Write a paragraph describing your reaction to it.

2. Which of the humans in the story did you like best and least? Why?

3. What do you think of Buck? Do you like the dog? Do you admire him? Or do you dislike him and what he does?

4. What is 'the call of the wild' which Buck follows? Do you think it is something that all dogs can feel? Is it a positive or negative thing?

5. Which part of the story did you enjoy most? Explain why.

B Comprehension

6 Explain who these people are and how they are connected to Buck. Write one sentence about each of them.

a Judge Miller — He was the man who owned Buck in California.

b Manuel ....

c The dog-breaker ....

d François ....

e Hal ....

f John Thornton ....

7 What things did Buck learn in his first few days in Alaska?

8 What is the significance of Spitz in the story?

9 What was the problem with Buck's feet, and how did François solve it?

10 What did the huskies do at nine, twelve and three o'clock each night in Dawson? Why is this important in Buck's development?

11 What helped Buck's team break the record on the way back from Dawson with François and Perrault?

12 What trick did Buck use to beat Spitz in the final fight?

13 When Buck lay by the fire who and what did he dream about? How is this connected to the title of the book?

14 Who bought Buck and his team when they got back to Skaguay? What were these men like?

15 How does Buck come to live with John Thornton?

16 Think of three times Buck helps John Thornton.

a ....

b ....

c ....

17 Who does Buck meet in the forest? What do they do together? Why doesn't Buck go with him?

18 What happens at the camp while Buck is away?

19 What does Buck do in the end?

C Characters

20 Describe the characters of the main humans in the story:

a) Manuel ....

b) François ....

c) Hal ....

d) John Thornton ....

21 Describe the characters of the main dogs in the story:

a) Spitz ....

b) Curly ....

c) Dave and Sol-leks ....

d) Skeet and Nig ....

22 With a partner trace the changes Buck makes throughout the story. What is he like at the beginning? What is he like at the end? Tell the class.

23 How does Buck react when he sees what has happened at John Thornton's camp?

24 How does Buck win the respect of the wolf pack?

25 Do you think the story has a happy ending for Buck? Why/why not?

26 Would you choose Buck to be your dog? Why/why not?

D Plot and Theme

27 Who tells the story? Buck? John Thornton? Another character? Who else? Explain the reason for your choice.

28 How is the story told? Tick (✓).

____ (a) With flashback, moving backwards and forwards from present to past.

____ (b) With a linear plot that moves directly from A to B to C.

____ (c) With a cyclical plot moving around a central event, always returning to it.

29 What is the effect of this way of story-telling? Think of the books and stories you have read. How are they told?

30 Which of the following themes is present in *The Call of the Wild*? Tick (✓). Find examples to illustrate each one.

____ (a) The cruelty of man

____ (b) Loyalty

____ (c) Man's greed

____ (d) Respect for nature

____ (e) The importance of our roots

31 How many years does the book cover?

32 What are the main events in the story? Write the events from the theft of Buck to when he joins the wolf pack.

The theft of Buck

Buck joining the wolf pack

33 Which of the following sentences describe the story best? Tick (✓).

____ (a) How a dog becomes wild.

____ (b) How a dog returns to its old, natural state.

____ (c) How humans mistreat dogs.

____ (d) How humans are unimportant for dogs.

34 What events in the story bring Buck closer to 'the wild'?

35 What does London mean at the end of the story when he says that Buck 'howls out the song of the younger world'?

36 Do you think that the story has a positive or negative ending? Explain your answer to a partner.

TEST

1 Read the text and then look at the sentences about holidays in the Yukon. Decide if each sentence is correct (✓) or incorrect (×).

HOLIDAYS IN THE YUKON

Would you like to see the home of the Klondike Gold Rush? Then visit the National Historical Park, and see what the gold miners' life was like! The seaside town of Skagway is a good place to stay, and it was the starting point for many of the miners. The weather is mild for most of the year, with no snow on the ground between March and October. The temperatures get up to nearly 21℃ from June to August; June and July also have very low rainfall.

There is much to do, especially if you enjoy walking in wild country with few people and lots of wildlife. You can watch seals and whales in the sea, and bears, moose and other animals in the forests. There are also many kinds of birds and flowers to see.

The National Historical Park offers a number of different guided tours with its rangers, and if you feel adventurous, you can hike up the famous Chilkoot Trail, which was used by the Gold Rush miners. It is difficult, even in summer, and you need to be an experienced and fit walker to do it; you also need to take the right camping equipment, clothing and food. You can check what is advised on the National Park Service website. One interesting thing is that if you hike up the trail from Skagway, like the miners, you will cross the border from the USA into Canada!

____ (a) Skagway is a good place to stay because of the weather.

____ (b) It snows in Skagway from November to February.

____ (c) The area is busy, lively and full of people.

____ (d) The National Historical Park is a good place to watch wild animals.

____ (e) The Chilkoot Trail is very easy for hiking in summer.

____ (f) You need special equipment if you walk the Chilkoot Trail.

____ (g) You go from Canada into the USA if you hike up the trail.

2 **Read the text below and chose the correct word for each space. Write 1, 2, 3 or 4 in the space.**

THE ALASKAN HUSKY

The Alaskan husky is not really a breed of dog like a German shepherd or a poodle, but a type of dog. They are bred as working dogs to (a) .... sleds. They typically weigh around 20 kg, and can have a coat of any (b) .... from black to white; it is usually short. Their (c) .... are usually brown or blue. The most important thing about an Alaskan husky is its speed, strength and endurance. Although husky dogs were first (d) .... in Alaska in 1577 by the English explorer Martin Frobisher, they were really developed in the late nineteenth century by the miners in the Alaskan Gold Rushes.

Alaskan huskies do not make good (e).................... in town houses and flats. Because they are working dogs and travel long distances, they need a lot of (f).................... and very good training. They are intelligent animals, and very easily get (g) ...., especially if they are left alone. They are good diggers, and can easily (h) .... from a garden. They are also natural hunters, and will (i) .... any small animals like cats, rats and even smaller dogs.

a	① push	② pull	③ run	④ ride
b	① shape	② size	③ color	④ height
c	① eyes	② ears	③ noses	④ teeth
d	① heard	② born	③ grown	④ seen
e	① animals	② dogs	③ pets	④ mammals
f	① exercise	② exercises	③ practice	④ jobs
g	① interested	② bored	③ excited	④ animated
h	① hide	② get lost	③ escape	④ jump
i	① find	② like	③ play with	④ chase

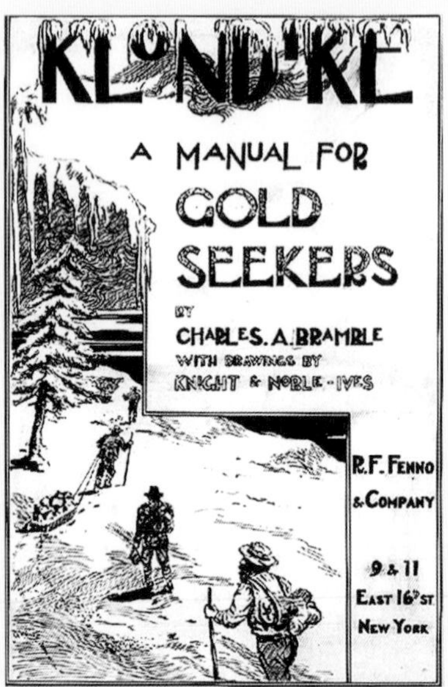

THE KLONDIKE GOLD RUSH

Find out the true facts about the Klondike Gold Rush which inspired *The Call of the Wild.* Answer the following questions, and then use your answers to write a report about it.

a) How much gold has been mined in the Yukon area since the first gold was found?

b) What happened in August 1896, and why was Keish (Skookum Jim Mason) important?

c) What problems were there in the USA that made so many people want to go and look for gold?

d) Where did people travel from to find gold in the Yukon? What sort of people were they?

e) What were the chances of finding gold?

- (f) Why did people have to take one ton of supplies?
- (g) Who checked the people arriving to look for gold?
- (h) Of the 100,000 people who went to the Yukon, how many actually got to the gold fields?
- (i) How did many people become rich at the time of the gold rush?
- (j) What were some of the most difficult things about the journeys they made through the Yukon?

Use the Internet to find the answers.

TRANSLATION

作者簡介

傑克・倫敦， 1876 年生於舊金山。他成長時期生活困苦，十歲就做了童工。他做過很多種工作，甚至是非法的事，而且還曾經流浪街頭。他利用空閒時間上圖書館閱讀，可以在裡頭待上好幾個鐘頭。

1894 年，他回返校園念書，並且出版了他的第一篇短篇小說《日本海岸的颱風》。接著，在 1896 年，他上了加州大學柏克萊分校，最後卻因經濟問題而輟學。

1897 年七月，他因克隆岱的淘金熱潮來到阿拉斯加。和很多淘金客一樣，他在那裡弄壞了身體，後來返鄉，以搖筆桿為職。他創作短篇故事，很快得到熱烈迴響。

1903 年，他寫了一部讓他留名青史的小說《野性的呼喚》。 1904 年，他出版第二部小說《海狼》。他用寫作所賺取的收入，在加州買了一個大莊園，他最後於 1916 年卒於此地。

他是一位多產的作家。從 1905 到 1916 年間，他出版了十八部小說、六本的短篇故事集、一部劇作，和各種非小說類的作品，其中還包含了一本自傳。在他去逝後，還出版了他的其他作品。

他知名的小說有《白牙》（1906 年）、《鐵蹄》（1908 年）、《馬丁・伊登》（1909 年）。然而，他在晚期時被指控剽竊他人所寫的新聞報導內容，然後再用自己的筆法改寫成故事。有人質疑這種寫作技巧是一種抄襲行為。

本書簡介

《野性的呼喚》（1903 年），被認為是傑克・倫敦最傑出的作品，名列美國經典文學之林。

故事中的主人翁是一隻叫巴克的大狗，他從生活愜意的加州，被偷賣到冰天雪地的克隆岱當雪橇狗。巴克面臨的是嚴峻無情的新生活，為了生存，他只得適應。他的雪橇隊，負責為前往冰冷北國的淘金客遞送郵件。

堅毅不拔的巴克 ，很快成為雪橇隊的領隊狗。隨著故事中的巴克在主人來來去去的過程中，他愈來愈接近自己原始的根源，「野性的呼喚」變得愈來愈強烈。

這篇故事探討了倫敦所喜愛的諸多主題。作者在前往克隆岱淘金時，隨身便攜帶了達爾文的《物種起源》一書。故事裡就強烈反映了達爾文「適者生存」的理論，並且無論是在動物還是人類的世界裡，適者生存的法則都同樣適用：為了生存，人類和動物都必須善用自己的力氣和大腦。

倫敦是一位因果決定論者，他認為生命決定於我們的遺傳與生活的環境。因此當巴克住在米勒法官的家裡時，他是一隻生活平靜悠哉的寵物，而他深藏的本能需要一定的環境才會被激發出來。在倫敦後來出版的《白牙》一書中，也可以看到相同的主題。

進入蠻荒之地

P. 15

巴克沒看報紙，所以不知道自己厄運將至。不只是他，從西雅圖到南加州，每隻肌肉結實、耐寒的長毛狗，都面臨同樣的命運。人們在北極區的地底下發現了金礦，吸引了成千上萬的人湧進，他們需要健壯且耐寒的狗來幫忙幹活。

巴克住在加州陽光明媚的一座大宅院裡，這是米勒法官的房子。這裡由巴克當家。巴克在這裡出生，轉眼已經過了四年。這裡還養了其他的狗，不過他們都住在狗舍或屋子裡，但巴克不是那種住在室內或是住在狗舍裡的狗。米勒法官的這一塊土地都歸他管轄，他在這裡稱王。他不只管那些走的、爬的或飛的動物，連人也是歸他管。

他父親葉莫是一隻大型的聖伯納犬，生前和法官形影不離；父親過世後，巴克繼承了父親的地位。他的體型沒有父親來得大，他只有六十公斤重，因他的母親雪珀是蘇格蘭牧羊犬。巴克養尊處優，他自恃不是看門狗，所以顯得恃才傲物。狩獵和各種戶外活動讓他肌肉結實，游泳讓他常保健康。

P. 16

上述就是巴克於 1897 年秋天的生活，值此之際，人們在克隆岱發現了金礦，來自各方的人馬紛紛湧向冰天雪地的北方。巴克不會看到這條新聞，也不知道那位叫曼紐的園丁助手心懷不軌。曼紐因為賭博，輸光了僅有的一點錢。有一次，趁著法官出差、法官的兒子忙著運動俱樂部時，曼紐幹出了壞勾當。他和巴克出門時，沒有人看見，巴克還以為只是出去散散步而已。也沒有人看到他們來到了火車站，那裡有個陌生人在等著，曼紐當場把巴克賣給他。

曼紐拿了一條粗繩子套在巴克的項圈下。巴克沒有反抗，因為他認識曼紐，不過等到繩子交到陌生人的手裡時，他狂吠了起來。套在脖子上的繩子緊緊勒住他，他喘不過氣來，憤怒地撲向陌生人。陌生人壓制住他，他仰躺在地上，脖子上的繩子被套得更緊。巴克這輩子還沒受過這麼惡毒的對待，這也是他生平第一次發這麼大的脾氣。之後他的氣力慢慢耗盡，不久就昏迷過去。火車進站時，他渾然不知自己被這兩個人丟進了行李車廂內。

P. 17

信任

• 巴克跟和曼紐走，是因為他信任曼紐，但曼紐背叛了他。你信任的人有哪些？你曾經被信任的人背叛過嗎？

巴克醒來後，聽到一聲汽笛鳴聲，知道自己身置何處，因為他常和法官搭火車。他睜開眼睛，眼裡充滿憤怒，他成了落難的大王。陌生人跳起來想抓住繩子，但巴克的動作更快，他一口咬住男子的手不放，直到再度被繩子勒昏過去。

男子手上包紮的手帕血跡斑斑，右腳褲管一路從膝蓋裂到腳踝。男子走進舊金山濱水區的一家酒吧，和酒吧老闆談話。

喉嚨和舌頭的劇烈疼痛，讓巴克頭暈目眩。他一次次被摔在地上，被勒得喘不過來氣，直到脖子上的銅項圈被剪斷。隨後，他們解開繩子，把他丟進一個籠子裡。

P. 18

他躺在籠子裡度過了一整夜，心裡非常憤怒。他不知道發生了什麼事，這些陌生人要對他做什麼？為什麼要把他關在這個小籠子裡？他很不安，有一種厄運到來的感覺。夜裡，他撲跳了幾次，期待眼前出現的是法官或法官的兒子，但看到的都是過來巡視的酒吧老闆。

巴克待的這個籠子被轉手了好幾次，和別的箱子一起裝上貨車，之後再裝上渡船，最後來到一個火車站，被安置在

一列快車上。他在開往北方的快車上度過了兩天兩夜，沒吃沒喝。他的怒火愈燒愈旺。他很想喝水，紓解一下腫痛的喉嚨和舌頭。他下了決心，決不再讓任何人拿繩子套在自己的脖子上。誰要是想再傷害他，他會跟他拚了命。他一雙眼睛變得通紅，他成了一個憤怒的魔鬼，整個面相都變了，連法官也會認不出他來。

兩天後，火車來到了西雅圖，巴克被卸下火車，送進一個四面都是高牆的小院子裡。那裡有一個穿著紅色毛衣的肥佬，他一手拿著小斧頭把籠子破壞掉，一隻手握著一根棍子。籠子的洞口被敲得偌大時，巴克跳出籠子，他像一個雙眼赤紅的魔鬼，衝向肥佬。

P. 20

然而，就在他一個騰空，轉眼要咬住肥佬時，棍子狠狠落在他身上，他第一次嚐到這種滋味。他的身體痛得翻騰，摔落地面。他這輩子還沒挨過棍棒，不

知道這是怎麼一回事。他發出刺耳的狂吠聲，再一次撲向肥佬，然後又再一次被打倒在地上。這時他才明白這到底是怎麼一回事，但他的憤怒讓他持續狂撲。就這樣，他被打倒在地十幾次。

最後，他再也沒有力氣撲起來，他的鼻子、嘴巴和耳朵滿是鮮血。肥佬從容地走過來，往他的鼻頭再補上一棒。這一擊痛徹心肺，他發出獅吼般的一聲咆哮，再度撲向肥佬，肥佬再朝他的下顎狠狠打下去，巴克被拋向空中，頭部和胸部往前摔落在地上。巴克爬起來做最後一搏，肥佬使出最後的狠招。最後巴克昏死過去，摔落地上。

「他不愧是一個馴狗專家！」運送巴克來這個院子的一個男人說。

巴克這時回過神來，但已經力氣頓失。他躺在地上，瞪著穿著紅色毛衣的肥佬。

「這隻狗叫巴克。」肥佬讀著酒吧老闆的信，說道：「好啦！巴克，我們剛剛小小的較量過了，最好到此為止了。你瞭解自己的處境了，乖乖聽話，一切就相安無事，要不然吃不完兜著走，懂嗎？」

P. 21

他一邊說著，一邊大膽地拍著那顆剛被他毒打過的頭。巴克豎起毛髮，但沒有反抗。肥佬拿水過來時，他埋頭便喝，還吃下肥佬親自餵食的一塊塊生牛肉大餐。

他被打敗了（他知道），但他沒有被擊垮。他明白到一點，面對拿著棍子的人類，他沒有勝算。他記取這個教訓，終身不忘。他學到了野蠻世界的第一課。

日子一天天過去，不斷有狗被送進來，有些狗很溫馴，有些狗和他一樣憤怒地咆哮。他目睹穿著紅色毛衣的肥佬，一次又一次將其他的狗馴服。巴克明白到，規矩是由拿著棍棒的人類所決定，他們是主人，必須服從，但他們不一定是朋友。

巴克心裡頭的滋味

- 巴克現在心裡頭的滋味如何？
- 他的感受是如何一路變化的？
- 你想，他接下來會遇到什麼樣的事情？

P. 22

時常有陌生人前來跟肥佬交談，他們會把錢交到肥佬手裡，然後帶走一隻狗。巴克想不透這些狗去了哪裡，為什麼都一去不回，他不禁對自己未來的命運感到不安。最後，有一個叫做「裴洛」的瘦小男人，他付了三百塊美金，挑上了巴克。他和另一隻叫可莉的溫馴紐芬蘭狗，一起被裴洛帶走。

這兩隻狗被帶上船，由裴洛和另一個叫「弗朗哥」的男人看管。弗朗哥是法國和加拿大的混血兒。這兩個人算是善待巴克，巴克雖然對他們沒有什麼感情，但還滿敬重他們的。他很快就發現到他們是正派人士，而且很懂狗，不會被狗給愚弄。船上還有另外兩隻狗，一隻是叫做「史比茲」的白色大狗，他很難對付，會偷巴克的食物；另一隻是叫「達夫」的狗，他很悶，沒什麼聲音，對什麼事情都提不起勁。

船一路往北行駛，天氣日漸寒冷。最後，船終於靠岸。弗朗哥把這些狗綁在一起，牽到甲板上。一踏上冰冷的甲板，巴克的腳就陷在一種白白軟軟、像泥土一樣的東西裡。他叫了一聲，往後跳。天空上落下更多這些白白的東西，他抖抖身子，但東西還是一直落在他身上。

他好奇地嗅了嗅味道，用舌頭舔了舔，那東西像火一樣，一下子就消失掉。他搞不清楚那是什麼，又舔了一次，結果還是一樣。一旁的人們看得哈哈大笑，他覺得很不好意思，但他搞不懂他們在笑什麼。這是他生平第一次看到雪。

棍棒與利齒的法則

P. 24

巴克上岸的第一天，是一場惡夢，隨時隨地都在給他震撼教育。他突然從文明世界，被拋進這個野蠻的世界，這裡沒有平靜，無法放鬆，片刻的安全都不可得。在這裡必須時時提高警覺，這裡的人和狗，跟城鎮裡的不一樣，這裡很野蠻，沒有法律這種東西，遵守的是「棍棒與利齒的法則」。

他第一次見識到狗可以打成這樣，初次體驗就教他畢生難忘。是可莉當了替死鬼，讓他保住了性命。那天，可莉向一隻愛斯基摩犬示好，這隻狗的體型只有一匹成狼的大小，個頭還不到可莉的一半大。但毫無預警地，他迅速撲過去，用利齒咬了一下，然後跳開；就這樣，可莉的臉從眼睛到下巴整個被撕裂。

在攻擊之後立刻跳開，這是狼的打鬥方式。事情還沒結束，三、四十隻愛斯基摩犬隨即衝過來觀看，把正在搏鬥的狗圍在中間，虎視眈眈，一聲不響地等待著。可莉衝向敵手，對方攻擊之後又立刻跳開。可莉再度撲過去，對手用很奇怪的姿勢，頂著胸部把她撞倒在地。可莉從此倒地不起。四周圍觀的愛斯基摩犬就等這一刻，他們擁向可莉，又吠又叫。可莉沒在群狗之中，發出痛苦的嗥叫聲。

P. 25

這一切始料未及的事情發生得太突然，巴克震驚不已。他看到在一旁觀看的史比茲露出笑容。弗朗哥這時跳進狗群，三個手持棍棒的男人一起幫他，狗群很快就跳散開來。而可莉倒在浸染了血跡的雪地上，早已斷氣。巴克時常會想起這一幕，這就是他所處的新世界，無所謂的公平遊戲。你只要一倒下，就是斷魂日，他得小心不能讓自己倒下。史比茲這時又露出笑容，巴克從此看他不順眼。

公平遊戲

- 巴克所說的「公平遊戲」是指什麼？
- 如果換作是你，你會對這種陌生而殘暴的世界做出什麼反應？

不久後，又有一件事情讓巴克很震驚：弗朗哥在他身上套上了挽具！他以前看過馬匹在工作時就是戴著那玩意，而現在他也開始拉車了！他拉著弗朗哥的雪橇去山谷的樹林，然後拉著一車的木材回來。他不喜歡這種差事，但他很精明，知道不能反抗。他雖然是新手，工作生疏，但他盡量做到最好。另外兩隻狗——史比茲在最前面帶頭，達夫的位置則最靠近雪橇——他們在弗朗哥和皮鞭的威嚇下，很快就把巴克調教好，讓他明白拉雪橇時的規矩。

P. 26

裴洛又另外買來了三隻狗，這支雪橇隊現在有六隻狗。其中的兩隻是一對愛斯基摩犬兄弟，分別叫做「比力」和「喬」；另外還有一條狗是年紀比較老的愛斯基摩犬，他是隻獨眼狗，叫做「索列克」，意思是「發怒的狗」。史比茲會欺負新來的狗，他會攻擊比力，卻不會對喬怎麼；索列克和達夫一樣，只想獨處，但巴克日後會見識到他們的生命力。

當天夜裡，巴克無法入睡。他想鑽進帳篷裡睡覺，但弗朗哥和裴洛對他又罵又扔東西，將他趕出帳篷。外頭寒風刺骨，他躺在雪地上，一下子就被凍得爬起來。他帳篷外繞著，發現無處不冰冷。他走回夥伴那裡，想看看他們是怎麼睡的。但令他很吃驚的是，他們都不見了！

P. 27

他落寞地四處尋找他們，當他走到帳篷旁時，前腳踏到的地方突然陷下去，原來那個點是比力蜷縮成一團、埋在雪下取暖睡覺的地方。巴克又學了一課。他選了一個地方，為自己挖了個洞。剎時，小小的洞裡立刻充滿身體的熱氣，他頓時便墜入夢鄉。

他一直睡到被營區的嘈雜聲吵醒才睜開眼睛。一開始，他想不起來自己身在何處，夜裡下過雪，他的身體整個被埋在雪堆裡。他很驚慌，還以為自己可能掉進陷阱裡，不過他接著往上直直一跳，就看到白天耀眼的陽光了。他眼前看到了營區，想起自己身處何方。從和曼紐散步，到昨晚為自己挖洞，所有的事情一幕幕回到眼前。

P. 28

弗朗哥一看到巴克，就大聲地跟裴洛說：「我就說嘛，巴克一定可以學得很快的！」

裴洛正經八百地點了點頭。裴洛是加拿大政府的信差，肩負遞送重要公文的責任，很需要最好的狗來幫忙，所以特別高興能找到像巴克這樣的狗。

另外又有三隻愛斯基摩犬加入這支隊伍，現在總共是九隻，他們很快被套好挽具出發。巴克很高興終於上路了，工作雖然辛苦，但他並不討厭。他很驚訝全隊的狗都生氣勃勃，尤其是達夫和索列克，他們一套上挽具就整個變得很不一樣，不再死氣沉沉。他們變得機靈好動，拉雪橇似乎成了他們生活的目標，也是他們唯一喜歡做的事。

達夫的位置最靠近雪橇，巴克排在他的前面，再前面的是索列克，其餘的狗又在他們更前面排成一路縱隊，一直到帶隊的史比茲。

巴克被刻意安排在索列克和達夫中間，以便訓練。巴克學得很快，達夫和索列克也很會教，他們透過利齒來教導巴克。一天下來，巴克便駕輕就熟，弗朗哥出鞭的次數也少了許多。

P. 29

這天要爬上峽谷，特別辛苦。他們穿越樹林帶的邊線，跨過冰河和數百尺深的雪地，翻越齊窟大山分水嶺，這個分水嶺是孤寂北方的一道屏障。

他們很快通過一連串的湖泊，深夜時分抵達泊涅湖前頭的大營區。那裡已經進駐了數千名淘金客，他們在那裡靜待春天，等待湖面融冰。疲憊不堪的巴克就在這裡的雪地上挖了個洞睡覺。

日復一日，巴克戴著挽具賣力地工作著。他們每天天未亮就啟程，一直到天黑了才紮營休息，然後吃點魚，鑽進雪洞裡睡覺。巴克很飢餓，狗一天一公斤鮭魚乾的食物量，並不夠他吃。其他的狗體重比較輕，而且過慣了這種日子，所以能維持良好的體力。

巴克發現，很快吃完食物的夥伴，會來偷吃他的份，所以他只得吃跟他們一樣快。他因為太餓，所以也學會偷吃別人的食物。他看到另一隻叫「派克」的新來的狗，他趁裴洛轉過身時偷了一塊培根。第二天，巴克如法炮製，偷了一大塊肉。他們發現了很生氣，但沒有懷疑是巴克偷的，而是由另一隻新來的狗

「杜柏」當了替罪羔羊。

初來到這個環境惡劣的北國，偷竊是巴克必須學習的生存技倆。他知道一定要調整自己來適應這個嚴峻的新環境，不然很快就會一命嗚呼。

P. 30

巴克的新生活

- 巴克過著什麼樣的新生活？
- 這和他以前的生活有什麼不一樣？
- 為了生存，他學到了哪些事？

巴克適應得很快：他的肌肉變得硬如鋼鐵；現在他什麼東西都可以吃下肚子裡；他的視覺和嗅覺也變得更敏銳，聽覺尤其更是異常靈敏，連在睡夢中也能聽到微弱的聲音，並且判斷出有沒有危險；他學會了用牙齒剔除腳趾間的結冰；口渴時，如果水面上結了厚厚的冰，他能夠用前腳把洞口的冰敲碎；他也學會嗅出風的動向，判斷出當晚會刮什麼風，所以他都能夠選一塊最安全的地方來挖洞睡覺。

他不僅從經驗中學習，他體內喪失已久的野性本能，也再度復甦。狗一代代長期被豢養下來所積存的習性，逐漸從他身上一點一滴地消失。要學會狼的戰鬥方式並不難，他的祖先們也是用這種方式戰鬥。當他在死寂的寒夜對著星斗仰天長嗥，就彷彿他的祖先們也正透過他聲聲悲號出來。

原始的獸性

P. 31

巴克的血液中流著強烈的原始獸性，尤其在這種險惡勞苦的生活中，他的這份獸性愈來愈強，暗中滋長著。他學會了精明，這讓他懂得自我控制。他不會和史比茲鬥，也不會做任何事去激怒他。

反之，史比茲只要一逮到機會，就會想要跟他大戰一場。這一定會是一場殊死戰。一天晚上，他們在雷霸湖畔紮營。這一晚很悽慘，大雪紛飛，疾風如刀，但天色這麼黑，所以即使四周是千仞懸崖，他們也只能就地紮營，裴洛和弗朗哥只得在結冰的湖面上生火、鋪床。

巴克在一塊峭岩下挖了要睡覺的洞，洞裡頭舒適又溫暖，但巴克不得不離開去吃飯。等到他吃完東西回來時，洞已經被史比茲霸佔了。到目前為止，巴克始終避免和史比茲正面衝突，但這次孰不可忍。他撲向史比茲，凶狠的舉動讓雙方都吃了一驚。

P. 32

這兩隻狗圍成一圈互相對峙，伺機出招。這時，突然發生了一樁意外事件，營區擠滿了從印地安部落來的飢餓的愛斯基摩犬，他們被食物的味道吸引過來，趁著巴克和史比茲戰鬥時悄悄接近。裴洛和弗朗哥拿著棍子衝到狗群裡，這些狗皆牙抵抗，食物的氣味讓他們瘋狂。有一箱食物被翻倒，二十幾隻餓犬立刻蜂擁而上，搶食麵包和培根。他們一方面被棍棒打得唉唉叫，一方向只管猛吃，直到地上什麼食物都不剩。

巴克以前沒見過這些狗，他們骨瘦如柴，目露凶光，張嘴露牙。他們餓得發瘋，非常駭人。巴克被三隻愛斯基摩犬圍攻，不一會兒，他的頭部和肩膀就有多處撕裂傷。巴克攻擊另一隻愛斯基摩犬時，他覺得有牙齒嵌進自己的喉嚨裡。這是史比茲，他從側面襲擊。

P. 33

裴洛和弗朗哥趕過來搭救，那群飢餓的瘋狗逃開，巴克這才掙脫出來。比力突破惡犬的重圍，往結冰的湖面逃去，後面跟著派克、杜柏和其他的狗。正當巴克要跟隨同伴殺出重圍時，史比茲又想向他攻擊過來。巴克知道，只要自己一倒下，就必死無疑。他看著史比茲，承受住他的攻擊之後，再追上夥伴逃走。

這九隻狗跑進樹林裡躲起來，每條狗身上都有好幾道傷口。天一破曉，他們一瘸一拐走回營地，掠奪者已經離去，裴洛和弗朗哥的心裡很氣。他們的糧食被吃掉了一半，現場一片狼藉。原本在檢查裝備的弗朗哥，轉而停下來檢查這些受傷的狗。

P. 34

到道森市還有六百公里的路程，裴洛急著啟程。這支受傷的隊伍這時來到了最難走的一段路——「三十哩河」，這段路讓他們有得受了。這條河水流湍急尚未結冰，只有在水流比較平緩的岸邊處結上一層冰，才能讓人行走。這三十哩路需要馬不停蹄地趕上六天，而且隨時一個腳步都可能讓人和狗喪命。

裴洛還是走在最前面探路，他跌進冰河裡十幾次，每次都只靠著自己手上的長竿橫抵住洞口，救回一命。氣溫零下五十度，天寒地凍的。每一次只要裴洛跌進冰河裡，他們就得停下來生火，讓他烘乾衣服，不然他可能會被凍斃。

但裴洛是個百屈不折的人，這也就是他會當政府信差的原因。他每天都危機重重，有一次，達夫和巴克連同雪橇一起掉進冰河裡，當他們被拖救出來時，已經奄奄一息，身體都凍僵了。他們得不停繞著火堆跑，一邊流汗，一邊讓冰融化，才能保住性命。

又有一次，史比茲掉進河裡，整支狗隊連帶被往下拖，幸好到了巴克的位置時，巴克、達夫和弗朗哥使盡全力往後拉，才沒讓雪橇掉進河裡。還有一次，隊伍前方和後方的冰層同時破裂，這時唯一的生路就是爬上陡峭的懸崖脫困。他們用一條長繩把狗一隻隻吊上懸崖，之後還要找出可以爬下懸崖的地方。這一天，他們沿著河只走了幾百公尺的路。

P. 35

裴洛和弗朗哥

- 裴洛和弗朗哥是什麼樣的人？請和你的夥伴，想出三個形容詞來分別形容他們。

他們抵達結冰堅硬的鐵絲林湖後，巴克一行狗已經精疲力竭。但裴洛為了彌補先前耽誤的時間，就要他們趕路。他們第一天走了五十公里，來到大鮭地；第二天走了也走了五十多公里，來到小鮭地；第三天走了六十公里，來到五指山山下。

巴克的腳不像愛斯基摩犬那麼硬，他一整天的路程走下來會痛得一瘸一拐。每次只要一準備搭營，他就會像死狗一樣癱倒下來，就算餓得要命，也不願挪身去吃東西，弗朗哥只好親自端到他面前。弗朗哥每天晚上也都會幫巴克的腳按摩個半個鐘頭，還用靴子上緣的皮幫他做了四個腳套，讓他減輕了不少痛苦。

有一天早晨，弗朗哥忘了幫巴克穿上腳套，他就躺在地上，四腳朝天，不肯上路，直到幫他把腳套穿上。他這個舉動逗得兩個人哈哈大笑。後來，他的腳底變得愈來愈堅韌，磨破的腳套也就隨手扔了。

P. 36

在毗里，有一天早上，在他們套上挽具時，一向很安靜的朵莉突然發瘋。她發出一聲長長的狼嗥，把其他的狗嚇得心裡發毛。接著，她撲向巴克。巴克沒見過有狗會發瘋成這樣，他嚇得拔腿就跑，朵莉在後面窮追不捨。弗朗哥吹起口哨，巴克氣喘噓噓地掉頭再跑回來。當巴克跑過弗朗哥的身邊時，弗朗哥拿著一把斧頭，朝著發瘋的朵莉的頭上擊去，朵莉當場斃命。

巴克爬到雪橇旁躺下，他精疲力竭，顯得很虛弱。這是史比茲的機會，他撲向巴克，連咬了他兩口，撕咬的傷口深可見骨。接下來就看到弗朗哥讓史比茲猛吃鞭子，這是這支隊伍到目前為止最慘烈的一次鞭打。巴克看在眼裡，痛快在心裡。

P. 37

「史比茲是個魔鬼！他終有一天會把巴克做掉。」裴洛說。

「那巴克就是魔鬼中的魔鬼！我一直在觀察他，我敢說——你聽好了，總有一天，他會發作，把史比茲啃掉，把他一口一口吐在雪地上！」弗朗哥回答說。

巴克和史比茲

- 和夥伴討論一下巴克和史比茲的關係。為什麼史比茲會這麼痛恨巴克？
- 弗朗哥說「他會把史比茲啃掉，把他一口一口吐在雪地上！」這是什麼意思？

從此以後，史比茲和巴克就一直處於備戰狀態。史比茲，身為雪橇隊的領隊狗，他覺得這隻奇怪的蘇格蘭犬威脅著他的地位。他看過很多蘇格蘭犬，他們都很軟弱，不是做得累死，就是凍死或餓死。但巴克卻不是這樣，他和那些愛斯基摩犬一樣強壯、野蠻、狡猾。他懂得潛伏，擁有野蠻世界的耐性。

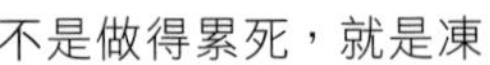

巴克期待來一場地位爭奪戰，這出自一種天性，而且他現在覺得身為雪橇狗是一種殊榮。他開始公然挑戰史比茲的領導權。

P. 38

有一回，派克在套挽具時沒有現身，史比茲去找他，就在他準備修理派克時，巴克從中介入。巴克撲向史比茲，把他撞倒，讓派克可以下手。巴克和派克就這樣聯手攻擊史比茲，弗朗哥跑過來對巴克抽鞭子，直到他願意住手。

他們一步步接近道森市，巴克繼續在史比茲和他想教訓的狗之間興風作浪，不過他學乖了，懂得選弗朗哥不在的時候下手。也因為這樣，這些狗愈來愈沒有紀律，除了達夫和索列克。巴克和史比茲之間的問題越演越烈，弗朗哥很明白，爭奪領導權的生死搏鬥遲早會發生。

只不過一直還沒有機會發生。他們抵達道森時，這場大戰還在醞釀著。在道森，人很多，有數不清的狗，巴克看到每一隻狗都在工作，好像狗生來就該工作似的。他們做著各種拖曳的工作，在加州，這是馬匹在做的工作。每晚到了九點、十二點和凌晨三點時，這些愛斯基摩犬會準時唱起詭異的夜歌，巴克也會跟著吟唱起來。這是一首古老的歌曲，和狼的血統一樣久遠——這是古老世界裡最早出現的一首悲歌。

P. 39

七天後，他們進入育空河道，啟程返回帝衣峽谷和鹽水鎮。裴洛這一批所要運送的郵件似乎特別緊急，他想來一趟今年度最快的送件。他有幾個有利的條件：經過七天的休息，狗都已經恢復體力；他們之前來道森所走的河道，上面的雪被後來的隊伍踩得結實了；另外，警方也在兩、三個休息處放了人和狗的糧食，所以這回他們可以輕裝上路。

第一天，他們一口氣趕了七十五公里的路；第二天，他們沿育空河直奔毗里。然而，這樣的速度讓弗朗哥有點吃力，因為巴克暗中主導著叛亂，破壞了雪橇隊的團結。這些狗開始欺負史比茲，他們會搶食他的食物，並且襲擊他。

P. 40

除了達夫和索列克，其他狗之間的關係也開始變化，他們常互相攻擊。弗朗哥知道這一切都是巴克在暗中搞鬼，巴克也知道弗朗哥洞悉這一切，不過巴克很狡猾，不會再當場被弗朗哥臟到。他套上挽具時會表現良好，因為他很喜歡這份工作；而暗中煽動同伴們打架，對他來說則是一種莫大的樂趣。

一天晚上，在塔基納河口吃過晚餐後，杜柏發現了一隻兔子，但他沒撲著。接著，全部的狗都跟著追逐起來。在幾

百公尺之外，另一個營地裡的五十隻愛斯基摩犬也加入追逐行列。兔子沿著河流下游奔竄，跑進山谷。兔子在雪地上跑起來很輕盈，而狗的腳會陷入雪地裡，跑起來很吃力。巴克率領狗跑在前面，但他無法抓到兔子。他一邊奔跑，一邊感到受到本能的驅使：他跑在最前頭，追著一個活生生的軀體；他渴望用牙齒取了他的性命，把鼻子埋進溫熱的鮮血裡；他體內深藏著的這些感受，將他喚回生命最初的時刻——這種感覺吞噬著他。

反之，史比茲卻像平常一樣冷靜地思考著。當巴克和其他的狗追著兔子跑向河流的拐彎處時，史比茲脫離狗群，抄進一處狹隘的地方。巴克沒有發現這條捷徑。就在巴克繞過河彎時，忽然看到史必司跳下來，在兔子的前方逮住兔子。兔子無法逃脫，狗的牙齒咬住牠的背脊，牠發出一聲淒厲的叫聲。一聽到這個叫聲，巴克身後的狗群亢奮得狂吠起來。

P. 42

巴克沒有跟著吠叫，也沒有停下腳步。他跑向史比茲，用他的肩膀撞史比茲的肩膀。他們在鬆軟的雪地上翻滾了幾圈，史比茲很快站起來，對著巴克的肩膀咬過去，然後迅速地跳開。

巴克知道，時機已經來臨。他們對著彼此繞圈子，互相咆哮，伺機而動。其他的愛斯基摩犬在一旁圍觀，鴉雀無聲。這一幕並不陌生、也不奇怪，事情一直都是這樣發展下來的。

史比茲的戰鬥經驗很豐富，從司畢次柏根到北極圈，橫貫加拿大，什麼樣的狗他都交手過，而且都成了他的手下敗將。他怒火中燒，但不會因此失去理智。他一心想置對方於死地，他也知道對手也想置他於死地。除非他做好被撲擊的準備，否則他不會撲向對方；他也不會展開攻擊，除非他能先防禦對方的攻擊。

P. 43

巴克想朝著這隻大白狗的脖子咬下去，但都無法得逞。他的牙齒想往肉的地方咬下去，但是都被史比茲的牙齒給擋回來。他們的牙齒互相碰擊，雙方唇破血流。巴克就是無法攻破史比茲的防線。他接著用各種方式撲向史比茲，想朝喉嚨咬下去，但都遭到反擊，而且史比茲都能成功跳開。這一次，他假裝要攻擊喉部，然後突然轉頭攻擊肩膀，想將史比茲撲倒。然而，史比茲每次都能跳開，而且在跳開之際反擊了他的肩膀。

史比茲毫髮無傷，巴克卻鮮血淋漓，氣喘如牛。戰況愈來愈危急，其他的狗像狼一樣靜靜圍成一圈，等著看哪一隻狗先倒下，就會撲殺過去。

P. 44

然而，巴克擁有一項卓越的天賦——想像力。他雖然憑著本能戰鬥，但也懂得運用頭腦。他撲過去，假裝要故計重施、做假動攻擊肩膀，但在最後一刻卻壓下身體，在落地前，他的牙齒就在史比茲的左前腳處，隨即傳來一聲骨頭被咬碎的聲音。就這樣，這隻白狗只剩下三條腿可以迎敵。巴克接連三次企圖把對方撞倒，接著再故技重施，咬斷史比茲的右前腿。史比茲強忍著劇痛和絕望感，拼命掙扎著站起來，然而，他看到靜靜圍觀的狗正一步步靠近他。

史比茲的氣數已盡，巴克準備給他最

後一擊。圍觀的狗如此逼近，巴克的背部可以感覺到他們的呼吸。這時，巴克一躍，史比茲便被他的肩膀推倒在地。在撒滿月光的雪地上，圍成一圈的狗變成一個個黑點，接著，史比茲就消失不見了。巴克站在一旁看著這一幕，這位勝利者，這頭原始的野獸，他完成了殺戮，油然生起一種滿足感。

打鬥

- 用你自己的話來說明何謂「打鬥」。
- 巴克是如何贏得打鬥的？
- 為什麼說巴克是「一頭原始的野獸」？

奪得領導權

P. 46

「怎樣，我說得沒錯吧？巴克是魔鬼中的魔鬼！」

這是隔天弗朗哥發現史比茲失蹤，而巴克又渾身是傷時說出的話。他把巴克拉到火堆旁，在火光下檢查他的傷口。

「史比茲打起架來真狠！」裴洛一邊看著撕裂的傷口，一邊說著。

「巴克比他狠上兩倍。這下我們日子比較好過了，史比茲沒了，麻煩也沒了。」弗朗哥回道。

史比茲

- 裴洛和弗朗哥為史比茲的死感到難過嗎？為什麼？
- 你想他們在期待這場打鬥發生嗎？

駕狗的弗朗哥把狗套上挽具，巴克隨即快步走到史比茲以前當頭的位置。弗朗哥沒注意到他，直接把索列克帶到這個大位上。依弗朗哥判斷，索列克是目前最適合當頭的狗。巴克憤怒地撲到索列克身上，把他趕回原地，自己站上了大位。

「你瞧瞧巴克，他把史比茲做掉，就以為可以取代他！走開！」弗朗哥大聲說道。

P. 47

但是巴克就是不肯讓出位置。弗朗哥拎起巴克的頸背，把他拉到一旁，再把索列克拉回位置上。這頭老狗並不垂涎這個位置，而且露出害怕巴克的樣子。待弗朗哥一轉身，巴克又走回來把索列克趕走。

弗朗哥火大了。「現在看我怎麼修理你！」他吼道，走回來時手裡多了根大棍子。

巴克想起那個穿著紅毛衣的肥佬，他怒吼著，身子往後退。駕狗人繼續準備出發的工作，他吆喝巴克說，要他等一下就要回到自己位在達夫前面的老位置上。巴克退了兩、三步，弗朗哥跟上去，他退得更後面。弗朗哥以為巴克怕挨打，便把棍子扔了。但巴克擺明了要革命，他想要當帶頭的，那是他的權利，是他贏來的。

裴洛也過來幫忙，他們想抓住巴克，結果折騰了一個鐘頭。巴克沒有跑開，只是保持距離不讓他們逮著。裴洛氣急敗壞，因為他們拖了一個鐘頭還沒出發。弗朗哥抓抓頭皮，裴洛聳聳肩，表示認輸了。弗朗哥走到索列克的旁邊，招呼巴克過來。巴克笑了，以狗特有的方式笑了，但仍保持一段距離。弗朗哥把索列克拉回原來的位置。弗朗哥又招呼巴克過來，但巴克仍然只是笑了笑，沒有過來。

「把棍子扔了吧！」裴洛說。

P. 48

弗朗哥照辦。巴克果然快步跑來，露出勝利的微笑，站上狗隊前頭的位置。他套好挽具，雪橇隊就啟程在河道上前進。

弗朗哥向來很欣賞巴克，但直到現在才見識到他的實力，巴克立刻肩負起領導責任。這份責任需要良好的判斷力和迅速的思考能力，在這方面，巴克表現得比史比茲更出色。然而，巴克最厲害的地方，是他很懂得如何讓隊友乖乖服從他的規矩。他讓愛偷懶的派克不敢偷懶，而且還做了史比茲做不到的事——給喬一番教訓。很快地，這支隊伍就恢復了秩序。在瑞克灘，加入了兩隻當地的愛斯基摩犬，提克和崑納。巴克用很快就讓他們乖乖服從，速度之快讓弗朗哥很驚訝。

「有哪條狗能跟巴克比？他值一千塊美金，哇！裴洛，你說是不是？」弗朗哥叫道。

裴洛點點頭。他已經打破時間紀錄，而且速度在還一天天加快中。路況良好，路面很硬又緊密，沒有下新雪，氣溫降至零下五十度後便一直維持穩定。

領導

- 弗朗哥和裴洛覺得巴克如何？為什麼？
- 你覺得一個好的領導者應具備哪些特質？和夥伴討論一位你覺得很有領導能力的人物。

P. 49

「三十哩河」的河面都結冰了，他們上一次花了十天的時間才走完這段路程，這一次卻只用一天的時間就走完全程。從雷霸湖到白馬灘，他們一口氣趕了九十公里的路。到了第十四天的晚上，他們爬上白山，在山腳思家威鎮和海上船隻的燈光下，沿著海岸斜坡下山。

這趟行程創新了紀錄，這兩週以來，每天平均可以走上六十公里路。

裴洛和弗朗哥在接下來的三天裡可威風了，他們的狗也備受推崇。然而這時來了公文，弗朗哥把巴克叫來身邊，抱著他哭了一場。就像其他來來去去的人一樣，弗朗哥和裴洛也將從此走出了巴克的生命。

一個有蘇格蘭血統的人，接管了巴克和隊友，將他們和另外十幾個狗隊合併，再度踏上艱辛的路程返回道森。這趟路不再輕鬆，他們後面拖的物品很重，每天都得吃力地工作著。他們是一支遞送郵件的隊伍，將世界各地捎來的消息帶給淘金客。

巴克不喜歡這份差事，但他仿效達夫和索列克以工作為傲的精神，他也會要求夥伴盡忠職守。這種日子日復一日，一成不變。伙夫在固定時間起床生火，弄早餐吃。接著有人拆營帳，有人給狗套挽具，趕在破曉前的一小時啟程。到了晚上就紮營，有人劈柴生火，有人幫伙夫提水提冰，接著是餵狗吃魚，這是狗一天當中最高潮的時刻，之後狗還會有蹓躂的時間。

P. 50

他們一行狗浩浩蕩蕩有一百多隻，當中也會有一些好戰份子。在和最凶猛的狗交鋒過三次之後，巴克成了老大，只要他咧出牙齒，其他的狗就會急忙躲開。

但或許，巴克最愛的還是在爐火旁閒躺著。有時，他會想起陽光明媚的聖塔克拉拉山谷裡米勒法官的大宅院，想起那裡的游泳槽和那些家犬。然而，更常浮現在腦海裡的，是穿紅色毛衣的肥佬、可莉的死狀、和史比茲的決戰，還有他吃過或是想吃的美味。

有時，當他躺在火堆旁時，他會神遊回到更原始世界裡。他看到身邊的是一個個頭矮小、全身毛茸茸的男人，男人會發出奇怪的聲音，而且害怕黑夜；男人穿得很少，只披著獸皮，唯一的武器是一根木棍，木棍的一頭綁著一塊石頭。在火光的外圍，巴克可以看到猛獸的眼睛，聽到他們在夜裡發出的聲音。這是另一個更原始世界的景象和聲音。

巴克的夢

- 巴克夢到了什麼？
- 巴克夢到的「原始世界」是什麼樣子的？
- 「一個個頭矮小、全身毛茸茸」是指什麼人？
- 在巴克的心裡，這個原始世界為什麼有這麼重的份量？

P. 52

拖送郵件很辛苦，沈重的工作讓他們精疲力竭。抵達道森時，他們個個都削瘦了。他們體力耗盡，起碼得休息個十天或一個星期才恢復得了。然而兩天後，他們就又拖著要送到外界的信件，沿育空河而下。狗都累壞了，駕狗人也在發牢騷，更慘的是，每天都在下雪，軟軟的路面，狗拖起東西來會覺得更吃力。所幸在整個路途上，駕狗人都很善待他們。

每天晚上，狗會比人先吃，而且駕狗人也會檢查狗群的腳。但狗的體力仍在消耗中。入冬以來，他們已經走了二千四百公里的路，這種路程連最強韌的狗也受不了。巴克一樣很疲憊，但他硬撐著，他監督同伴工作，並且維持紀律。

達夫的情況最不好，駕狗人找不出他的毛病，應該是身體內部出了什麼問題。當他們抵達喀峽沙洲時，達夫病得頻頻跌倒。駕狗人把他的挽具拿下，由索列克頂替他位於雪橇前的位置。他們讓達夫自由地跟在雪橇後跑，趁機休息一下。但這對達夫來說是一種折磨：他不要別人頂替他的位置。

P. 53

他想辦法跟上雪橇隊，直到隊伍再度停下來。這時駕狗人看到達夫站在雪橇的前面，那是他專屬的位置。駕狗人彼此討論了一下，他們知道，狗不管再累再病，也寧可鞠躬盡瘁，死而後已，而不願意被排除在工作之外。討論到最後，駕狗人幫達夫再套上挽具，讓達夫站上原來的位置，然後出發。他們一路前進著，達夫不時地跌倒，或是身體痛得不時發出哀鳴聲。

隔天早上，達夫爬向自己的位置，但他已經虛弱得無法上路。這是同伴們見到他的最後一幕：他躺在雪地上直喘息，兩眼依依不捨地望著他們。他們一直能聽到他哀淒的叫聲，直到拐進下一個彎路口。蘇格蘭駕馬人這時慢慢走回剛離開的營地，大夥靜默無語，接著傳來一聲槍響。駕馬人很快歸隊，鞭子又霹啪響起，雪橇的鈴聲叮噹作響，雪橇向前直奔而去。剛剛發生了什麼事情，巴克知道，所有的狗也都知道。

生存

- 達夫發生了什麼事情？為什麼？
- 你覺得這樣的結局公平嗎？
- 討論一下「適者生存」的說法。

挽繩和雪道

P.54

離開道森一個月後，巴克和隊友拖著鹽水鎮的郵件，抵達了思家威市。巴克原本八十公斤重的體重，掉到只剩下七十公斤，有些狗的狀況更慘。派克和索列克的腿受傷，杜柏則是傷到肩膀。每一隻狗的腳底都磨破了。這樣長時間做這麼吃重的工作，他們疲憊不堪。他們用不到五個月的時間，就跑了三千七百公里的路程！

駕狗人期待能有一個比較長的休息時間，他們走了一千八百公里的路，也只休息了兩天。這麼多男人來到克隆岱，

他們的家鄉有那麼多的妻子、親人和情人，所以有堆積如山的信件，此外也有很多的公文。一批從哈德遜灣來的狗，頂替那些累得無法再上路的狗，這些被換下來的狗隨後會被賣掉。

第四天早上，兩個美國佬買下了巴克、隊友和他們的挽具。這兩個人叫做「賀爾」和「查爾斯」。查爾斯是一個中年人，他的眼睛不太好，常會流出眼水。賀爾年約二十，腰帶上掛著一支大大的手槍和一把獵刀。這兩個人在這裡顯得格格不入，像他們這種人怎麼來會到北方，匪夷所思。巴克和隊友來到新主人的營地，他看到營地裡亂七八糟的。他還看到一個做梅瑟蒂的女人，她是查爾斯的妻子，也是賀爾的姊姊。這是一個家族。

P.55

巴克看到他們手忙腳亂地著手拆帳篷，把東西搬上雪橇。捲起來的帳篷比正常的體積大了三倍，錫製的碗盤都還沒洗就收起來。梅瑟蒂繼續在兩個男人之間走來走去、忙東忙西，嘴裡叨叨唸著沒閒過，一下埋怨，一下出主意。

P.56

巴克的新主人

- 巴克的新主人是什麼樣子的？
- 如果你是巴克，替這樣的主人工作，你會作何感想？為什麼？
- 你想接下來會發生什麼樣的事？

有三個男人走過來看他們，彼此哈哈大笑著。

「你們的行李太重了，要是我，就會把帳篷留下。」其中一個人說。

「怎麼可能！沒帳篷怎麼睡？」梅瑟蒂大叫說。

「都春天了，天氣不會再變冷了。」男人答道。

她搖搖頭。查爾斯和賀爾把最後一批東西裝到堆積如山的雪橇上去。

「這樣拖得動嗎？」其中一個男人問道。

「有啥不行？」查爾斯不悅地反問。

「看起來有點頭重腳輕。」那人輕聲地回答。

查爾斯轉過身，盡量把捆繩往下拉緊。

「當然啦，那些狗是可以整天拖著這些東西跑。」又有一個人說道。

P.57

「那當然。」賀爾轉身向狗，吆喝道：「走！出發！」

所有的狗使勁拉了一會兒後便鬆了下來。他們根本拉不動雪橇。

「這些懶惰的畜生！看我的！」他一邊叫罵，一邊準備揮鞭。

梅瑟蒂出面阻止，她叫道：「哦，賀爾，不可以這樣。可憐的東西！」她把賀爾手中的鞭子搶下來，說：「你要保證你不會揍他們！」

「你哪懂什麼狗啊，你別管，他們懶得很，不打就不走，他們就吃這一套，不信你可以問那幾個人。」弟弟說。

梅瑟蒂看著那幾個人，想得到他們的認同。

「這些狗累壞了，如果你想知道，我就告訴你，他們需要休息！」其中一個人回答。

「休息個屁啊！」賀爾說。

梅瑟蒂這時護著她弟弟，不理會陌生人，說道：「別理他！駕狗的是你，你覺得應該怎麼做，就怎麼做。」

賀爾再度向狗揮鞭子，狗又再次使盡全力、壓低身子往前拉，但雪橇仍一動也不動。試了兩次後，他們氣喘噓噓，但雪橇還是紋風不動。鞭子又咻咻地落下，梅瑟蒂眼裡轉著淚珠，她跪到巴克前面，兩手抱住他的脖子。

P.59

「你們好可憐啊，好可憐啊！你們為什麼不用力拉呢？那樣就不會被打了。」她憐惜地哭叫著。巴克不喜歡她，

但他此時心情很不好，也就不想抗拒她，就當她是今天苦差事的一部分吧。

在旁邊圍觀的其中一個人，終於說道：「你們會怎樣我是不管啦，我是看在狗的份上才跟你們說，你們幫忙推一下雪橇就行啦，雪橇底結冰啦。」

他們聽了建議，又做了第三次的嘗試，賀爾揮著鞭子打狗，這時超載的雪橇底破冰移動了起來。這條路在前方一百公尺處拐進一個下坡路，然後通到大馬路上。要維持這種頭重腳輕的雪橇平穩前進，就算是經驗老道的人駕馭起來也不是件容易的事。他們做了個轉彎之後，雪橇就翻倒了，有一半的東西被摔了出去。狗沒有停下腳步，重量變輕的雪橇跑得歪歪斜斜的。

他們那樣對待狗，又這樣超載，讓這些狗很生氣。巴克帶頭跑著，其他的狗一路跟著。賀爾叫著：「快停下！停下！」但這些狗不理會。賀爾的腳被絆到摔了下來，雪橇從他身上輾過；狗繼續狂奔著，沿途掉落在馬路上的東西，給思家威市添了熱鬧的氣氛。

P. 60

當地的好心人攔住狗，幫忙把散落的東西撿起來，然後勸他們說：如果你們想去道森，就要扔掉一半的東西。賀爾一家人勉強聽進去了。他們架起帳篷，整理所需裝備。當他們取出罐頭食品、毛毯、帳篷和一大堆碗盤時，圍觀的人哄堂大笑。梅瑟蒂看到自己的衣服也要扔掉，難過得哭了。到了最後，她連必備衣物也扔了。

東西扔完後，行李還是很可觀。查爾

斯和賀爾出去多買了六條狗回來，現在這支隊伍總共有十四隻狗。然而新添的狗不是很優良，他們好像什麼都不會。巴克和夥伴們很不屑他們。巴克很快教會他們守在自己的崗位上，告訴他們什麼事是不可以做的，卻無法教會他們什麼事是應該做的。他們也不適應挽具和雪道。這個陌生的新環境，對他們其中大部分的狗來說都很難適應，而且他們以前也沒有被這樣惡劣地對待過。

和這些無可救藥的狗工作，原來的狗還是太過操勞。情況看起來不是很妙，但兩個男主人卻很興奮，覺得很神氣：他們擁有一支十四隻狗的雪橇隊。他們看過很多在道森來來去去的雪橇隊，從沒見過哪個隊伍能擁有十四隻狗。

在北極，見不到十四隻狗的隊伍是有原因的：因為一個雪橇載不了十四隻狗的糧食！

查爾斯和賀爾不懂這道理。他們拿筆計算，一隻狗要吃多少食物？這麼多隻狗又需要多少食物？他們需要帶上多少天的糧食？他們覺得這是很好琢磨出來的。

P. 62

這趟行程

・你想這一行人和狗會遇到什麼問題？和夥伴討論一下。

隔日近午時分，巴克領著長長的隊伍走在大街上。這些狗剛出發就疲憊不堪。鹽水湖和道森之間的路途，他們已經來來回回走了四趟。疲乏的巴克一想到又要踏上一樣的旅程，就覺得更痛苦。他無心工作，其他狗也一樣，新來的狗很膽小，而且所有的狗都對主人沒有信心。

巴克覺得這兩個男人和這一個女人什麼都不懂，幾天下來，也可以看得出來他們什麼也學不會。他們做事毫無章法，要花了大半夜的功夫才能搭好一個不像樣的帳篷，早上又得花大半天的時間來拆帳篷。他們的行李打包得亂七八糟，常常要停下來調整，有好幾次，一天跑下來都跑不了十五公里。他們每天連一半的路程進度都跑不了，而他們是用這種進度來計算狗食的。無可避免地，食物一定會不夠吃。

P. 63

甚者，他們還給狗吃額外的份量，冀望他們可以因此跑快一點。離減食的日子，愈來愈近。那些新來的狗胃口很大，再加上原來的狗太累太虛、胃口沒那麼好，賀爾就給新來的狗兩倍的食物量。除此之外，梅瑟蒂因為覺得這些狗很可憐，也會偷偷背著賀爾偷拿魚乾給狗吃。不過，巴克這些狗需要的倒不是食物，而是休息。雖然他們是慢慢前進，但沉重的行李耗損了他們的體力。

減食的日子，終於來到。這一天，賀爾意識到他們已經吃掉了一半的狗食，然而他們才走了四分之一的路程，而且接下來沒有地方可以買狗食。於是他一方面削減食物量，一方面加長每天所跑的路程。減少狗的食物量，這種政策很好實施，但是，當主人每天早上都搞得亂七八糟，卻要他們走多一點路，那這就是辦不到的事情了。

最先喪命的杜柏。他受傷的肩膀一直沒有治療，情況日益惡化，最後賀爾只好用手槍擊斃他。那些新來的狗無法適應食物被減半，很快地就死了六隻狗。

P. 64

此外，這些人本身也遇到了問題。他們全身痠痛，脾氣變得很暴躁：肌肉疼痛，骨頭疼痛，心臟也疼痛。他們動不動就發脾氣，查爾斯和賀爾老是在吵架，彼此計較誰做得多、做得少。梅瑟蒂有時站在老公這邊，有時站在弟弟那邊，這一家人就這樣一路上吵吵鬧鬧。火也還沒生，搭營只搭了一半，狗也還沒餵，他們就光顧著互相指責。

梅瑟蒂滿腹心酸，她是個溫柔美麗的女子，向來嬌生慣養。如今她不想再管那些狗了，她全身疼痛，疲憊不堪，所以執意要坐雪橇。她是很美麗很溫柔沒錯，但她的體重也有八十公斤重。對這些又累又餓的狗來說，簡直是雪上加霜。她坐了幾天，直到全部的狗都跌在地上、拉不動雪橇為止。查爾斯和賀爾求她下來用走的，她就哭著說他們冷酷無情。

P. 65

梅瑟蒂

- 如果你是梅瑟蒂，你的心情會如何？為什麼？
- 你會給梅瑟蒂什麼建議？

他們自身難保，所以也就顧不了受苦受難的狗了。當他們抵達五指山時，狗糧已經耗盡。他們用賀爾腰帶上的手槍，跟一個印地安人換了一塊結成冰塊、重沒幾公斤的馬肉。這個食物滋味不佳，咬起來像在吃鐵塊，而不是吃肉。

這些日子以來，一直是巴克步履踉蹌地走在前頭帶隊，但這是一場惡夢。他拉得動就拉，拉不動就倒在雪地上，直到棍棒和鞭子把他打到站起來為止。他的皮毛早已失去光澤，整個瘦成皮包骨，令人鼻酸；然而，巴克是不會放棄的。

P. 66

其他六個同伴也是同樣的情況，他們是一批行屍走肉的狗隊，對於鞭子或棍棒早已麻木不仁，鞭打的疼痛感變得遙遠而模糊。雪橇停下休息時，他們就癱在原地；當棍鞭落下來時，他們才又甦醒過來，掙扎著站起身子，踉蹌邁進。

有一天，比力再也爬不起來。賀爾的手槍已經賣掉，就用斧頭對準比力的頭砍下，把屍體拖出來拋在路邊。巴克和夥伴親眼目睹了這一幕，他們知道下一個可能就會輪到自己。接下來撒手的是崑納，現在他們一行只剩下五隻狗：喬、派克、索列克、提克和巴克。

這是春光明媚的季節，但是沒有狗或人會去留意這件事。凌晨三點，天空就泛白，一直到晚上九點，都還有日光。長日裡，陽光終日燦爛，冰凍多時的大地開始復甦。每一座山都會傳來潺潺的流水聲，和冰雪掉落的聲音。這兩個男人、一個女人和幾隻狗，卻在這片生意盎然的大地上，如死亡隊伍般地緩緩前進。

P. 67

一路上，狗不停地跌倒，梅瑟蒂坐在雪橇上不時哭泣，賀爾滿口粗話，查爾斯不時流著眼水，就這樣，他們蹣跚來到白河河口處的約翰・桑頓營地。他們一停下來，幾隻狗就像斷了氣一樣地倒下來。桑頓聽著他們的問題，簡短地回答了一下，三言兩語提出建議。他很清楚，這些人不會把他的話聽進去。

「在思家威時，他們說冰開始融化，要我們先等等看再說。他們還說我們到不了白河，現在我們不是到了嗎？」賀爾說。

「他們說的沒錯。我老實告訴你，就算把阿拉斯加所有的黃金都給我，我也不想拿自己的性命開玩笑。」桑頓說。

「才不呢！我們要去道森！起來，巴克！快起來！」賀爾說。

他拿著鞭子，一隻隻狗輪流鞭打。除了巴克，其他的狗都站了起來。巴克靜靜躺在原地，賀爾不斷地抽打他，但他既不哀號，也不掙扎。桑頓好幾次忍不住想開口說話，但他還是改變主意。

桑頓

- 你想桑頓開口想說的話是什麼？
- 要是你，你會想跟賀爾說什麼？

P. 69

這是巴克第一次抵死不從，這讓賀爾很火大，換拿棍子來打他。巴克感受到一種厄運，他的腳底能感受到冰層愈來愈薄，他嗅到災難即將降臨在主人想要踏上的冰層之上，所以抵死不從。他已經吃那麼多的苦，早已奄奄一息，這種皮肉之痛再也傷害不了他。棍棒不斷揮下來，他生命的火焰愈來愈小，幾乎熄去。棍棒下的這個身體變得好遙遠，彷彿不再屬於他。

這時，在無預警的情況下，約翰・桑頓突然發出野獸般的聲音，然後撲向賀爾，將他撞退了幾步。梅瑟蒂放聲尖叫。桑頓護在巴克前面，他壓抑怒氣，氣得無法言語。

「你再打那隻狗，我就殺了你！」桑頓終於哽咽地擠出這句話來。

「這是我的狗！讓開！不然我就殺了你！我要去道森！」賀爾一邊擦掉嘴角的血，一邊說道。

桑頓站在賀爾和巴克中間，沒有讓開

的意思。賀爾抽出獵刀，梅瑟蒂驚聲尖叫，哭了起來。桑頓用拿在手上的斧頭柄，往賀爾的手敲過去，把獵刀打落在地上。賀爾想彎腰撿起刀子，桑頓又敲了他一下他的手，然後自己撿起刀子，把巴克的挽具割斷。

賀爾敵不過，而且姊姊跑過來抱住他。再說，巴克都奄奄一息了，也拖不了雪橇。幾分鐘後，他們啟程沿著河往下走。

P. 70

巴克聽到他們離開的聲音，抬眼望了望，他看到當頭的是派克，索列克在最後，中間的是喬和提克。他們一跛一跛地蹣跚前進，梅瑟蒂坐在負重的雪橇上，賀爾拉著雪橇，查爾斯則搖搖晃晃地跟在雪橇後面。

巴克望著他們遠去，桑頓蹲在旁邊，用粗糙而溫暖的手檢查看他有沒有骨折。還好巴克沒有骨折，只是餓壞了。這時，雪橇隊已經走了半公里遠，人和狗在冰塊上緩慢移動。然而就在此時，他們看到雪橇突然翻覆掉落！他們聽到了梅瑟蒂的尖叫聲，看到查爾斯想轉身往回跑，可是接下來整塊區域的冰破裂，這些狗和人就消失在眼前，只剩下一個大窟窿。桑頓和巴克彼此對看著。

「可憐的傢伙！」約翰・桑頓說著。巴克舔了舔他的手。

巴克

・如果你是巴克，你會怎麼想？
跟夥伴說說。

摯愛

P. 72

巴克終於得以放鬆。在春天的長日裡，他躺在河邊，看著水流，聽著鳥鳴和大地的聲音，體力逐漸恢復。踏過了四千五百公里路，能好好休息一番，是最稱意的事。他的傷口慢慢復原，卻也跟著變得懶散了。他骨頭上的肌肉又重新長出來。他也結交了新朋友，像是愛爾蘭小獵犬絲吉特、大黑狗尼格，他們都是約翰・桑頓原本就養的狗。而巴克，他給了約翰・桑頓無比的愛。

這個人救了他的命，而且他還是那種夢寐以求的主人。他對待這些狗，就像對待自己的孩子一樣。他只要看到狗，就會跟他們打招呼，然後坐下來說說話。巴克可以在他腳上躺上幾個鐘頭，然後抬頭望著他，捕捉他臉上的表情變化。

巴克很怕會失去約翰・桑頓，他之前的主人來來去去。然而，僅管他深愛著桑頓，也會謹守規矩，表現文雅，但北方生活所激發的原始野性，仍留在他的骨子裡。他是一頭野獸，來自荒野，現在坐在約翰・桑頓的火爐旁。

P. 73

他的臉和身體傷痕累累，這是戰鬥的印記。他打架的狠勁一如以往，只是現在會用更聰明的方式來進行。他不和絲吉特或尼格較勁，他們太善良了，更何況他們又是約翰・桑頓的狗。至於其他陌生的狗，都得立刻在巴克面前俯首稱臣，不然就得為了活命和可怕的敵手決戰。巴克很冷酷，連對垂死的對手都從不留情。他謹記教訓，明白事情沒有中庸之道：不是稱雄，就是稱臣；不是殺敵，就是得被殺；不是吃掉對方，就是被對方吃掉。這是法則，巴克所遵循的就是這條法則。

巴克的改變

- 故事一路下來，巴克有了哪些改變？
- 他現在變成了什麼樣的一隻狗？

P. 74

巴克坐在約翰・桑頓的爐火邊，這是一隻胸膛寬厚、一口白牙的長毛狗。然而在他身後，有著各種狗、狼狗和野狼的身影，他們呼喚著巴克，讓他和人類的關係漸行漸遠。森林深處響起一聲呼喚，每當他聽見這一聲呼喚，他莫名地就覺得應該離開爐火旁，奔入森林。但在這種時候，他對約翰・桑頓的愛會再把他拉回來。不過，他只為桑頓而留，其他的人他都不看在眼裡。

桑頓的生意夥伴漢斯和彼特，很了解巴克和桑頓的關係。

有一天，彼特這麼說：「要是我，我決不會在巴克的面前對桑頓動手。」

年關將近時，在色寇城，有一件事情印證了彼特的想法。有一個叫做黑伯頓的人，他是一個脾氣暴躁的危險份子。他和一個菜鳥年輕人起了爭執，桑頓介入勸解，巴克則在角落裡看著。這時伯頓出期不意地對了桑頓出了重重一拳，將他打飛去出了。

突然，圍觀的人聽見一聲怒吼，接著就看到巴克撲向伯頓的喉嚨。伯頓伸出手臂擋掉，救了自己一命，但身體仍被撲倒在地上。巴克鬆開咬住手臂的牙齒，再次朝著喉嚨進攻，咬破了他的喉嚨。人群湧上來把巴克趕走。在一位醫生在幫忙檢查伯頓的傷口時，巴克仍在一旁盤桓，他咆哮著，想再找機會攻擊。

P. 76

大家都認為巴克不是胡亂攻擊人類，所以後來沒被處罰。此後，巴克聲名大噪，名氣傳遍阿拉斯加的所有營地。

隔年秋末，桑頓和兩個工作夥伴駕著窄船行駛在湍急的河流上。當時桑頓的人在船上，漢斯和彼特在岸邊拉條長繩來固定船，以免船被急流沖走。

當時巴克就站在岸邊，憂心地看著主人。突然，一陣急流沖向船隻，繩子一個被拉直，桑頓就被拋進了河裡。巴克立刻躍入水中，來到主人的身邊。桑頓抓住巴克的尾巴，巴克隨即奮力往岸邊游去。

但湍急的水流又將他們沖走，他們就要被沖到最危險的岩石區河段。桑頓好不容易抓住河裡的一塊岩石，而巴克則吃力地往岸邊游去，彼特和漢斯出手抓住他，把他拖上岸。

他們接著在巴克的肩膀上套上繩子，讓他游到岩石邊的桑頓那裡。但水流又將他沖走，他差點溺斃，幸虧彼特和漢斯及時把他拉出水中。桑頓撐不了太久，他繼續拚命游向桑頓。桑頓抓住他的脖子，彼特和漢斯收繩將他們兩個拉回岸上。他們在水流和岩石間被打得滿身是傷，巴克斷了三根肋骨，不過他總算救回了主人的性命。

危險

- 你曾經遇到什麼危險的情況嗎？是誰救了你？
- 你曾經救過誰嗎？和你的夥伴說說你的心情。

P. 78

那年冬天，巴克在道森又有了另一項事蹟。這個晚上，桑頓來到酒吧裡。吧裡有人在誇耀自己的狗能獨自拉動三百公斤的雪橇，另一個叫做馬休森的人，則吹噓自己的狗能拉動四百公斤。

「這算什麼！巴克能拉動五百公斤的雪橇。」桑頓說。

「你是說他能掙破結冰、拉動五百斤，然後走上一百公尺？」馬休森問。

「這也沒問題。」桑頓淡淡地說。

「那我跟你賭一千塊美金，賭他拉不動。錢在這！」馬休森說罷，砰一聲把一袋沙金扔在吧檯上。

實際上，桑頓也不確定巴克做不做得到，他只是覺得他應該做得到。但即使如此，要拉動這樣的重量，還是很驚人的。此外，不管是他，還是彼特或漢斯，他們都沒有一千塊錢可以押注。

「我現在外頭就有一輛雪橇，上面有十袋五十公斤的貨，我們現在就可以來比。」馬休森說。

桑頓望著酒吧裡那些正盯著他看的人們，這時他看到一個淘金發了大財的老友。

「你能先借我一千塊嗎？」他小聲問道。

「好啊。但我覺得你的狗應該拉不動。」老友一邊把錢放在吧檯上，一邊說道。

P. 79

馬休森的雪橇上裝了十袋五十公斤的麵粉。雪橇停在嚴寒的天氣中停了兩個多鐘頭，凍得都結冰了。很多人過來圍觀，打賭巴克是不是拉得動。賭巴克拉不動的人數比是三比一，馬休森於是又另外加碼兩千塊。但桑頓和夥伴只有兩百塊，就賭馬休森的六百塊美金。

於是巴克戴上挽具綁上雪橇。巴克很亢奮，他意識到自己要為桑頓做一件大事。巴克現在的狀況很好，圍觀的人也都看得出來，但人們還是不認為他拉得動。桑頓走向巴克，兩手捧著他的頭，在他耳邊悄聲說：「巴克，我也同樣愛你。」

P. 80

桑頓站起身子，往後退了幾步，說：「巴克，開始吧！」

桑頓喊道：「往右！」巴克於是奮力往右邊擺動，搖動貨物，接著傳來冰裂的聲音。

「往左！」桑頓又命令道。巴克於是往左邊重複剛剛的動作，又聽到冰裂聲。雪橇下的結冰已經裂開了。

「現在，往前拉！」桑頓喊道。巴克低著頭，胸口貼近地面，開始拉雪橇。一開始，他的腳在雪地上打滑，後來沉重的雪橇開始一寸一寸地往前滑動，平穩地前進著。在旁屏氣凝神觀看的群眾，這時開始叫囂起來。當巴克拉完一百公尺，群眾們一陣狂呼。

桑頓跑向巴克，跪在他的旁邊，他們頭頂著頂頭，來回互相移動。桑頓最後站起身來，臉上滑下了兩行淚。

聲聲呼喚

P. 82

巴克只用了五分鐘的時間，就幫約翰・桑頓進帳了一千六百塊錢。有了這筆錢，主人和夥伴們就可以去尋找傳說已久的金礦。有很多人去尋找那片金礦田，其中有不少人有去無回。桑頓、彼得和漢斯帶著巴克和其他六隻狗出發，他們駕著雪橇沿育空河走了一百公里，再轉入四都河。他們往上流前進，最後來到高山上的源頭溪流。

約翰・桑頓不害怕荒野，他深入蠻荒，想到哪兒就到哪兒，想待多久就待多久。他沿途打獵時，總是從容不迫。就算一時獵不到東西吃，他也只管上路，心想反正遲早都找得到吃的。也因此，這趟路程所載的大都是彈藥和工具。

對巴克來說，能夠踏上未知的旅程，沿途打獵打漁、摸路前進，是一種無止盡的喜悅。他們有時可以接連幾個星期持續前進，有時又會紮營駐足許久來尋找金礦。他們有時會挨餓，有時又可以飽餐一頓。在夏日之際，他們砍伐林木做成木筏，這時人和狗都會扛著行囊，乘筏橫渡碧綠的山湖，或是在不知名的河流上，時而順流而下，時而逆流而上。。

P. 84

他們踏遍這片杳無人煙的荒野，這個地方在地圖上找不到，但如果傳說中的金礦是真的，那這裡以前就有過人跡。他們在這裡探尋了一個夏天和又一個冬天。

當春神再度來臨，他們還是沒找到傳說中的金礦，不過倒是在一個山谷的河流裡發現了金沙。他們駐足此地，每天可以淘洗出的金沙金塊，達數千元美金之多。他們每天不停地工作，把金子裝在皮袋裡，每袋重達二十五斤，一袋袋堆在他們搭起的棚子外頭。

在這種時候，狗派不上用場，巴克便成天在火堆旁沈思。那個個頭矮小、全身毛茸茸的男人，愈來愈常浮現在他的腦海裡。他現在無事可做，就常常躺在火堆旁，跟著這個男人在記憶裡的另一個世界裡神遊。

這個毛茸茸的男人擔驚受怕，總是四

下張望著，隨時準備好一遇到危險就要逃開。他會和巴克悄悄地通過森林，有時候他會跳到樹上，在樹枝之間盪來盪去，從不會失手，和在地上一樣的得心應手。

伴隨著這些畫面，巴克還聽到來自森林深處的聲聲呼喚。他內心裡有一種莫名的渴望，渴望著某種連他自己也不清楚的東西。有時他會跳起來，然後失蹤個幾個鐘頭。他會沿著乾涸的河道走去，望望鳥兒，聽著各種聲音，判斷各種跡象，像人們在翻閱書本那樣地判讀環境。他會尋找那個總是在聲聲呼喚他的神祕東西，不管是清醒還是在睡夢中，它總是在召喚著他。

P. 86

呼喚

- 「那個呼喚著他的神祕東西」，你想是什麼？
- 那是一種像說話聲那樣的真正聲音，還是別的東西？
- 想一想這本書的書名，然後和夥伴討論一下。

一天夜裡，巴克突然從睡夢中跳起來，嗅著空氣。他聽到森林深處傳來的呼喚聲，聲音有點像長長的嗥叫聲，但又不像是愛斯基摩犬的叫聲。他跑過人們正在睡夢中的營地，奔進森林。他離呼喚聲愈來愈近，腳步不自覺地放慢。他每一步都小心翼翼，最後來到林間的一處空地，在那裡看到一隻瘦長的灰狼。灰狼挺立身子、鼻子仰天地蹲坐在那裡。

巴克沒有出聲。灰狼停止嗥叫，嗅著氣味。巴克走進空地，他的每個動作都兼帶威脅和示好。然而，灰狼一見到他就跑掉。巴克隨後追上他，把他堵在角落裡。他轉過身，對著巴克，牙齒咯咯作響。

巴克沒有發動攻擊，只繞著他打轉，用友好的態度趨前靠近。灰狼一方面覺得奇怪，一方面感到害怕，因為巴克的體型比他大了三倍。這時，灰狼抓住機會又逃開。他們繼續追逐。灰狼被堵在角落裡好多次，終於卸下心防，他發現巴克並無惡意，便用鼻子和巴克相互嗅聞。他們一起嬉戲。後來灰狼要前往別的地方時，他要巴克也一起跟過來。

P. 87

他們接著上了山谷，來到一處平原，那裡有連綿的森林，還有很多溪流。他們肩並肩奔跑，時間一個鐘頭一個鐘頭地過去，直到東方泛白、大地溫暖起來。巴克很興奮，因為他和這位狼兄同奔而去的地方，就是呼喚聲響起的地方，他知道自己終於回應了呼喚聲。遠古的記憶浮現腦海，那是他在另一個世界的經歷。如今他再次體驗往昔曾做過的事：在遼闊的天空下，雙腳站在的大地上，自由地奔馳。

他們在溪邊停下來喝水。這時，巴克想起了約翰・桑頓，便坐了下來。灰狼繼續朝呼喚聲響起的地方奔去，他跑了沒一會兒，就折返回來。他嗅一嗅巴克的鼻子，催他上路。然而，巴克卻掉過頭去，開始慢慢往回走。灰狼發出哀鳴聲，跟在他旁邊走了半個多小時。最後，灰狼坐下，鼻子仰天嗥叫了一聲，音聲很淒涼。巴克繼續往前走，他愈走愈遠，嗥叫聲愈離愈遠，直至消逝。

巴克的決定

- 巴克為什麼決定離開灰狼？
- 你有過難以抉擇的經驗嗎？那是什麼事？為什麼難以決定？跟夥伴聊聊。

P. 89

巴克奔回營地時，約翰・桑頓正在吃飯。他熱情地撲到桑頓身上，將他撲倒在地，朝他的臉上舔著。接下來連續兩天兩夜，巴克未曾離開營地一步，而且不讓桑頓跑出他的視線範圍。巴克跟著桑頓去上工，盯著他吃飯，晚上看著他上床，早上看著他起床。然而，兩天之後，森林的呼喚聲又再度響起，而且變得更加急切。巴克的心裡又躁動了起來，他想著灰狼，想著山谷外那片天地，想著和其他的狼一齊奔跑。他又開始在森林中遊蕩，但灰狼沒有回來。灰狼那聲悽涼的叫聲，也未曾再響起。

巴克開始徹夜不歸，而且一離開就是好幾天，但他還是看不到灰狼的蹤影。他沿途獵食，步履輕盈，不知疲倦。他會在河裡抓鮭魚吃，還曾在一場大戰中擊斃了一隻大黑熊。

他嗜血的欲望愈來愈強烈。他變成了掠殺者，靠捕食動物為生，只吃活生生的東西。他靠著自己的力量和能耐，獨自獵殺食物。在強者適存的艱困環境裡，他可以悠遊其中。除了棕色的鼻頭和胸前那片白毛，他看起來儼然就是一隻大野狼。無論是在體能或心理上，他的生命力都處在巔峰。他的觀察、判斷和反應，可以在瞬間同時完成。

P. 90

「再也找不到像他這樣的狗。」約翰・桑頓有一天如此說道。當時他們三個人正望著巴克步出營地。

他們看著巴克走出營地，但他們看不到巴克走進森林後急遽變化的樣子。巴克會頓時變成一頭野獸，像貓一樣悄悄前進，來無影去無蹤。他懂得如何在樹叢之間藏身，他會攫走窩裡的鳥，咬死熟睡中的兔子，逮住準備爬上樹的松鼠，或是在開闊的池塘裡抓魚。魚游泳的速度遠不及他快。

那年秋天，來了麋鹿群。麋鹿群從寒冷的山區往山谷遷徙，巴克獨力做掉了一隻中等大小的麋鹿，然而他一心想

要的目標，是體型更大、更難獵殺的動物。有一天，他在山谷上發現了一群數量二十幾隻的麋鹿群，當中有一隻體型特別大的雄鹿。雄鹿站起來的身長，足足有兩公尺高，這正是巴克求之不得的對手！雄鹿搖擺著大鹿角，鹿角張開的距離超過兩公尺寬。他看到巴克時，發出了怒吼的聲音。

P.91

巴克第一件要做的事，是把雄鹿引出鹿群，但這件事並不好辦。每次只要巴克激怒大雄鹿望他這邊衝過來，就會有幾個年輕雄鹿跑過來，幫助大雄鹿趁機歸隊。然而，就像所有的掠食動物一樣，巴克很有耐性。他可以花大半天的時間跟隨他們，然後從四面八方做攻擊，把雄鹿和鹿群隔開。白天漸逝，會跑來護大雄鹿的年輕雄鹿，亦隨之減少。

夜幕低垂時，移動的鹿群步入了黑暗之中，巴克從中阻隔，大雄鹿無法歸隊，只能單獨面對巴克。大雄鹿重達一千一百五十公斤，他這一生威風凜凜地活了大把歲數，經歷過無數的奮戰，如今，眼前這隻身高只到他膝蓋的動物，竟要取他的性命，讓他命葬齒下！

巴克對這隻大雄鹿緊跟不捨，而且不讓雄鹿停下來休息，或是喝水進食。雄鹿如果想逃跑，巴克就從容地在後頭追著；雄鹿如果停下腳步，巴克就躺下來休息。只要雄鹿想吃東西或喝水，巴克就會猛烈攻擊他。

雄鹿的大頭顱愈垂愈低，步伐也愈來愈慢。他會垂頭呆呆地長時間站著，這時巴克會趁機喝水。巴克在一旁靜待，突然，他感覺到這個區域會有一場變化，將會有不同種類的動物踏上這塊土地。他並未聽到或看到什麼，但他嗅出了將會有一場變化。他決定等他解決掉這頭麋鹿，就要去探個究竟。

P.92

到了第四天的傍晚，大雄鹿終於被他扳倒在地。他獵殺了大麋鹿後，留在原地進食和睡覺，休息了一天一夜。他恢復了精神和體力之後，穿過陌生的土地，轉頭返回約翰・桑頓的營地。他輕鬆地邁開大步，一個鐘頭一個鐘頭地持續前進，直直地朝著家的方向走去，完全不會迷路。

P. 93

他愈向前跑，就愈強烈感受到這片土地上的新騷動。有外來的新生命進入了這片土地，它和這一帶夏季裡的生命不同。小鳥和松鼠在吱吱喳喳說著這件事，連風也在低訴著。有好幾次他停下腳步，嗅著空氣，聞出消息，他的判斷讓他加快前進的腳步。他察覺到危險，有一場災難正在發生。最後他越過山頂，準備跑下營地所在的山谷。他步步為營。

P. 94

巴克的第六感

- 你想巴克察覺到什麼了？
  發生什麼事了？
- 你想結果會怎樣？

在離營地五公里遠的地方，巴克發現了新的足跡，令他寒毛直豎。足跡通向約翰・桑頓的營地，他的每根神經都緊繃著。他加緊腳步，悄聲地飛奔下去。他敏銳地觀察眼前所有的細節，這些細節訴說了整個事件——除了結局。他留意到林子裡一片死寂。他嗅到了東西，他把頭轉過去，看到身旁躺著尼格。尼格已經斷氣，他被一支箭射穿了身體。

不一會兒，他又看到路上有一隻奄奄一息的雪橇狗。巴克沒有停下腳步，繼續跑著。這時營地隱約傳來一陣聲音，歌聲起起落落。

P. 95

巴克匍匐爬到營地的空地旁，他看到漢斯滿身都是箭地趴在地上。他抬眼看，眼前的景象讓他瘋狂。他任自己的憤怒壓過狡黠和理智。因為是摯愛的約翰・桑頓，所以他失去了理智。

依哈族印地安人這時正圍著營地跳舞，突然傳來巴克的怒吼聲。人們轉頭看到一隻陌生的動物，像一陣狂風似地向他們撲過來。他撲向酋長，把他的喉嚨撕裂，接著繼續攻擊周圍的人。沒有人能抵擋得住他，他竄到人群中，毫不留情地猛撕猛咬。依哈人朝巴克射箭，但箭都失準，反倒射到了其他的印地安人。人們嚇得倉皇逃入樹林，以為巴克是惡靈降臨。

P. 96

巴克追進樹林裡，像獵鹿一樣把他們一個個搏倒。這是依哈人黑暗的一日。他們四下散開，各自逃命，等到一個星期後，幾個劫後餘生者才重聚在一起清

點傷亡人數。巴克在厭倦追逐之後，返回景況悽慘的營地。他發現彼特死在毯子裡，而地面上桑頓冒死搏鬥的痕跡仍清楚可見。巴克仔細地嗅著這些痕跡，循著氣味來到一個深池邊，忠心護主到最後一刻的絲吉特就躺在那裡，而掉進混濁水裡的，是約翰・桑頓。巴克嗅著桑頓的氣味循跡前進，但氣味來到水邊就斷掉。

一整天，巴克不是坐在水塘邊，就是煩躁地在營地周圍徘徊。他見過死亡是怎麼一回事，他也明白約翰・桑頓已經死去。這留給他一種痛苦的空洞感，像飢不得食那樣的痛苦。有時，在看到依哈人的屍體時，痛苦會消失一下下，而且會有一種自豪的感覺。他竟把人類給做掉了，而人類是最高的攻擊目標。他嗅了嗅這些屍體。人類這麼容易就斷氣，比解決一隻愛斯基摩犬還容易。如果沒有弓箭或棍棒，人類根本不是他的對手。從現在起，他對人類沒有顧忌了，除非人類手上有弓箭或棍棒。

夜幕降臨，一輪滿月從樹梢升起，高掛夜空。巴克躺在池子旁哀悼沉思，這時森林中一股新的騷動驚擾了他。他站起身來，一邊聽著聲音，一邊嗅著氣味。遠處傳來一聲模糊而尖銳的叫聲，接著一聲聲響起。慢慢地，嗥叫聲愈來愈靠近，愈來愈清晰。巴克聽清楚了那就是深藏在記憶中另一個世界的呼喚聲。

P.99

他走到空地的中間，駐足聆聽。就是那種呼喚，那種聲調起起伏伏的呼喚，如今更加深深地吸引著他。這一次，他

已經準備好要順從這個呼喚。約翰・桑頓已經逝去，他和人類最後的連繫已經斷裂，人類和人類的夢想，再也無法挽留住巴克。

野性的呼喚

- 現在巴克有了什麼樣的改變？為什麼？
- 你想他接下來打算怎麼做？

狼群為了獵食，他們跟在遷徙的麋鹿群後面，越過溪流和樹林，來到了巴克所在的山谷。月光下，狼群如銀色的水流湧進空地裡。巴克像尊雕像一動也不動地站在空地中央，等著狼群過來。看到巴克偌大的身軀紋風不動地站著，狼群安靜無聲，屏息了片刻。接著，一隻狼撲過來，巴克迅雷不及掩耳地做出反擊，咬斷了狼的脖子。狼在他的眼前斷

氣之後，巴克又靜靜地站立著。接著，又有三隻狼輪番發動攻擊，卻旋即匍匐退回，他們的喉嚨和肩膀被撕裂，渾身是血。

巴克的舉動，引來狼群的集體攻擊。巴克的動作十分敏捷，他迅速地竄來竄去，又撕又咬。為了避免腹背受敵，巴克且戰且退。他退到水塘，然後再沿著淘金客所築的高堤，繼續後退。最後他退到一個三面都有屏障的角落，在這裡只要對付前方的敵人就可以。

P. 100

印面而戰的巴克和他們打了半個鐘頭之後，不敵的狼群敗退。狼群裡有的躺著、有的站著，直盯著巴克看。就在這時，有一隻瘦瘦的灰狼，他小心翼翼、用示好的態度走向巴克。巴克認出了他，他就是那個曾經和他一齊奔跑過一天一夜的兄弟。他輕輕地嗥叫了一聲，巴克也叫了一聲回應他，然後和彼此互碰鼻子。

一隻疤痕累累的老狼走上前來，也和巴克彼此嗅了嗅鼻子。之後老狼坐下來，對著月亮仰起鼻子，叫了長長一聲狼嗥，其他的狼也跟著坐下來仰天長嗥。這次，巴克清清楚楚聽到了呼喚聲。他也坐下來，對天長嗥。隨後他走出角落，狼群半友好、半粗野地將他團團圍住。狼群的領袖長嗥一聲，帶著狼群步入樹林裡。巴克也發出嗥叫聲，跟在狼群裡，和他的灰狼兄弟並肩前進。

巴克的故事講到這裡，差不多要落幕了。然而不久之後，依哈人發現森林中的狼種起了變化，一些狼的頭部和鼻子上長了棕色的毛，胸前還有一條道白色的毛紋。更令人詫異的是，依哈人開始傳述說，在狼群的前面有一隻「鬼犬」帶頭跑著。人們很害怕這隻鬼犬，因為他比人還要狡猾。他會在寒冬裡跑進他們的營地偷東西，破壞捕獸器把食物取走，也會殺掉他們養的狗，而且連他們最勇猛的戰士，他也毫無畏懼。

P. 101

更令人毛骨竦然的是，有些獵人離開營地後就一去不回。等到他們被找到時，喉嚨已經被撕破，附近雪地上留著的腳印，比狼的腳印要大上許多。每到了秋天，依哈人在追捕遷徙的麋鹿時，有一處山谷是禁地，他們從不進入。他們圍著火堆，說著鬼犬為何選擇那座山谷作為棲息地時，無不神傷。

P. 102

鬼犬

- 「鬼犬」是指誰？
- 你的文化裡有什麼傳說或故事？
- 你聽過的傳說有哪些？和你的夥伴分享一下。

然而，依哈人並不知道，每年夏天都會有個訪客來到山谷。那位訪客是一隻有著漂亮毛皮的大狼，他看起來像隻狼，但和其他的狼又不太一樣。他會獨自穿越溪流和森林，來到樹林間的一塊空地上。那裡有一道黃濁的水流，從陳舊的鹿皮袋中慢慢流出，滲入地底。這隻狼會在這裡沉吟許久，在離去前會發出一聲哀傷的長嘷。

但他並非一直獨來獨往。在漫長的冬夜裡，當狼群追逐獵物進入低窪的山谷時，在黯淡的月光下，可以看到他的身影跑在狼群的最前面。他的體型很大，他強韌的喉嚨唱出新世界的歌曲——野狼之歌。

ANSWER KEY

Before Reading

Page 10

1 (possible answers)
Carnivorous, Friendly, Dangerous, Useful, Intelligent, Loyal, Faithful. Domesticated, Strong

3 1. c 2. f 3. e 4. a 5. b 6. d

Page 11

5
a) Alaska belongs to the United States of America.
b) Alaska is located in the north west of Canada.
c) The climate is cold. The south of Alaska is milder and wetter while the north is colder with snow and ice all year around.
d) Polar bears, brown bears, wolves, eagles and foxes are Alaska's native animals.
e) The first inhabitants of Alaska arrived from Asia during the Ice Age.

6 People discovered gold there.

Page 12

11 1, 2, 3

Page 13

13 1. d 2. c 3. f 4. a 5. g 6. b 7. e

Page 21

- Buck has lost his sense of trust. He feels that man is now someone who has to be obeyed.
- His feelings have changed because he has been physically beaten and he has watched other dogs being beaten.

Page 25

- He means a sense of respect and treating each other in a decent way.

Page 30

- Buck's new life is difficult. He works hard and uses different strategies to survive as well as possible in the hostile environment.
- His old life was comfortable; this life is totally different.
- He has learned how to dig a hole in the snow to keep warm while sleeping, behave while pulling the sled and steal food without being caught in order not to be hungry.

Page 35

- Perrault and François are hard workers who are not afraid to take risks and determined to get to their destination.

Page 37

- Buck and Spitz have got a bad relationship. Spitz is very aggressive towards Buck and tries to hurt him at every opportunity. He seems to hate Buck because he perceives him to challenge his position as the lead dog. François thinks Buck will eventually beat Spitz.

Page 44

- Buck wins the fight by tricking Spitz.
- He is called 'the primitive beast' because he used his primitive instincts to win the fight.

Page 46

- No, they are not sorry because Spitz caused trouble.

Page 48

- They think that Buck is very good because he is a good and instinctive leader, and the dog team works well under him.

Page 50

- Buck dreams about a primitive man.
- The 'earlier' world is a world thousands of years ago.
- The 'short, hairy man' is a primitive man.
- This world is important to Buck because by following his instincts he is getting closer and closer to an older and more primitive way of life.

Page 53

- Dave had been left to die because he was too weak to continue the journey.

Page 56

- Buck's new owners are two men and a woman. The men are out of place and the woman is unhelpful. They are unorganized.

Page 73

- Buck has learned how to survive in even the most hostile circumstances. He now knew how to survive in any situation.
- He is strong and intelligent with a highly developed survival instinct.

Page 86

- It is Buck's natural instinct calling to him.

Page 87

- He decides to leave the wolf because he feels loyal to Thornton.

Page 94

- Buck senses that something terrible has happened.
- The camp has been attacked by Yeehat Indians and all the men are dead.

Page 99

- Buck no longer feels the need to stay in a civilized society as Thornton is dead. He is free to become wild.

Page 102

- The 'Ghost Dog' is probably Buck.

After Reading

Page 106

6

b) Manuel was one of the men who helped in Judge Miller's garden. He sold Buck at the start of the story.
c) The dog-breaker is a man in Seattle who beats dogs in order to make them tame.
d) François is French-Canadian who buys Buck along with another man and takes him on his first journey across Alaska.
e) Hal is a young man who buys Buck along with Charles and Mercedes.
f) John Thornton saves Buck from Hal.

7 Buck learned how to survive.

8 Spitz is Buck's antagonist in the story. Buck learns to defend himself from Spitz and to beat him.

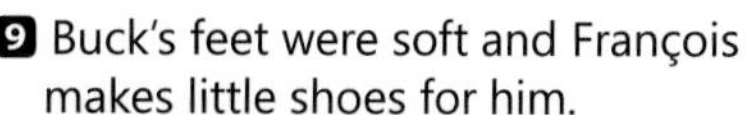

9 Buck's feet were soft and François makes little shoes for him.

10 The huskies howled at these times. This helps Buck get in touch with his primitive side.

11 They made the record run because the weather conditions were good.

Page 107

12 Buck pretended he was going to jump and bite in the usual place but at the last minute he attacked Spitz in a different way.

13 Buck dreamt of an ancient primitive world that represents the 'Wild' in the title of the book.

14 A Scotsman and his mates bought Buck and the team. The men worked hard but they were fair.

15 John Thornton sees Hal hitting Buck and he intervenes and saves him.

16

a) He defends Thortnton from Black Burton in a fight.

b) He saves Thornton when he falls into the river.

c) He pulls the sled with 500 kilos of flour in order to win a bet.

17 He meets a wolf and they run through the forest together.

18 The camp is attacked by Yeehat Indians and all the men are killed.

19 In the end Buck becomes wild.

Page 108

20 (possible answer)

a) Manuel is dishonest and greedy.

b) François is fair and is a hard-worker.

c) Hal is disorganized and bad-tempered.

d) John Thornton is fair and respectful.

21 (possible answer)

a) Spitz is aggressive and ambitious.

b) Curly is friendly but weak.

c) Dave and Sol-leks want to be left alone.

d) Skeet and Nig are good-natured.

Page 109

22 (possible answer)

a) At the start of the book Buck is strong and good-natured. He belongs to Judge Millar and has an easy comfortable life. At the end of the book he has developed his survival instinct to the full and has returned to the primitive beast that dogs once were.

23 Buck rushes at the Indians like a hurricane attacking and killing them.

24 He wins the respect of the pack by defending himself and fighting them off.

Page 110

27 The story is told by a third person narrator who is not in the story.

28 b

29 This gives us a sense of Buck's development and how events effect and change him.

30 (possible answer)

a) The dog-breaker, Hal

b) Buck's loyalty to John Thornton

c) Manuel sells Buck in order to pay his debt.

d) Buck realizes they should not cross the frozen lake.

e) Buck feels the call of the wild (his roots) as something strong and natural.

31 The book covers a period of a little over a year.

Page 111

32 (possible answer)

- Buck's arrival in Alaska.
- Buck's first journey with François and Perrault.
- Buck's fight with Spitz and becomes the leader of the team.
- Buck starts to dream about the past.
- Buck is sold to Hal, Charles and Mercedes.
- John Thornton saves Buck.
- Buck hears the 'call of the wild'.
- John Thornton is killed.

33 (possible answer) b

34 Buck's learning to trust and use his instincts, his dreams and his meeting with the wolf.

35 He means that Buck is still not in touch with his wilder, primitive side.

Test

Page 113

1

a) √ b) √ c) X d) X e) X f) √ g) X

Page 115

2

a) 2 b) 3 c) 1 d) 4 e) 3
f) 1 g) 2 h) 3 g) 4

國家圖書館出版品預行編目資料

野性的呼喚 / David A. Hill 著 ; 安卡斯 譯 . 一初版 .
一 [臺北市] : 寂天文化， 2012.7
面； 公分 .

中英對照

ISBN 978-986-318-011-1 (25K 平裝附光碟片)

1. 英語 2. 讀本

805.18 101010890

■原著 _ Jack London ■改寫 _ David A. Hill
■譯者 _ 安卡斯 ■校對 _ 陳慧莉 ■封面設計 _ 蔡怡柔
■主編 _ 黃鈺云 ■製程管理 _ 蔡智堯
■出版者 _ 寂天文化事業股份有限公司 ■電話 _ 02-2365-9739 ■傳真 _ 02-2365-9835
■網址 _ www.icosmos.com.tw ■讀者服務 _ onlineservice@icosmos.com.tw
■出版日期 _ 2012年7月 初版一刷（250101）
■郵撥帳號 _ 1998620-0 寂天文化事業股份有限公司
■訂購金額600（含）元以上郵資免費 ■訂購金額600元以下者，請外加郵資60元
■若有破損，請寄回更換